# The Trouble
# With Harry

# The Trouble With Harry

JACK TREVOR STORY

**Allison & Busby**
*Published by W.H. Allen & Co. Plc*

An Allison & Busby book
Published in 1989 by
W.H. Allen & Co. Plc
Sekforde House
175/9 St John Street
London EC1V 4LL

First published by T.V. Boardman in 1949

Printed in Great Britain by
Courier International, Tiptree, Essex

ISBN 0 85031 825 4

# Contents

# A Place for the Dead

The small boy named Abie climbed the woodland path that led to Sparrowswick Heath. His body lay at an acute angle with the steep and stony way, a toy gun was clutched firmly beneath his left arm. You could tell, by the expression on his face, that he knew where he was going and why. You could tell that he knew this path and where it led; that it held no terrors for him, even though the trees crowded thick and leafy on all sides, further than he could see or the sun could penetrate. You could tell that this was *his* hunting-ground; he did the scaring around here; it was not the things in the dark woods that Abie feared, but the things that feared Abie. Abie was four; there was a strong, square look about his body, clad in long dungarees; he had a desperate set to his russet face, and the watered parting of his hair, running, as it did, half on the right-hand side of his head then cutting across and finishing up on the left-hand side, betrayed an adventurous spirit. Also Abie had the gun.

Up above the fringing woods the heath stretched out fine and beautiful and golden in the hot summer sunshine, spread with a ground fog of man-high bracken in all its pleasing shades of green. Here and there the bracken was broken by glades of silky grass, fine as a woman's hair and as inviting. Standing solemn and silent on the hills and in the valleys and on the slopes were the big trees; the oaks, beeches, chestnuts, birches and ash. All between them walked like children the young trees. Little scrubby oaks and upstart ash; prickly broom, blackthorn, rhododendron and sweet chestnut. And elegant little silver birch children standing sparse-leaved and open-branched with the just-so-ness of an exclusive window display.

Sparrowswick Heath was out of sight and out of sound of the world. A secret, remote place, safe from wheels. A place for the living and for the dead. On this particular afternoon a place for the dead.

Also it was a place of bungalows; incongruous, cheaply built. They stood at all kinds of funny angles down in the wood from where young Abie had come. They had been put there, deliberately and commercially, by a man named Mark Douglas.

Abie left the dark tunnel of the woodland path and came out into this golden country, his ears instant for the sounds of the big game that crowded the forests of giant fern. His small feet fell silently on the short, springy turf, and he walked with a special, wary step of his own invention.

Suddenly there came a thundering, roaring explosion that split open the soft bumbling silence and set all things quaking and shaking. Especially Abie. Abie knew it was the new captain out after game – but still! Abie turned around twice, quickly, and then fled into the bracken as swiftly as any game.

Presently he was sitting in one of the grassy glades, walled in by the bracken and listening. His face was raised to the patch of chalk-blue sky which was so far above him as to be of little importance, and his eyes were big and round with his concentration. The new captain was a plump and jolly man and Abie knew he would not willingly shoot him. Nevertheless, he also knew that the new captain would be out after rabbits and a small boy creeping through the bracken was not so very unlike a rabbit.

There came another shot. This time closer, and the little boy thought he heard the sound of it whistling over his head. He reached a decision. He decided to retreat and leave the game to the new captain. Abie had all the time in the world for shooting, being still less than school age, whereas the new captain often had to go to town and an afternoon like this might well be precious to him.

Abie travelled through the bracken on his stomach. It was not a comfortable mode of progression, for the gun had to be dragged somehow and the stubbly stems of last year's growth prodded him incessantly.

Just before he reached the pathway that led back to the woods he heard a commotion in the bracken ahead. A sudden burst of noise. Human exclamations and grunts and feminine indignation. The man's voice was subdued as if by intense feeling; the woman's voice sounded muffled as though by a cloth or a hand. Abie was not interested in the sounds, but he knew he must avoid them. He had a pretty shrewd suspicion what he would find if he crawled in the same direction for the next two minutes. A nest of lovers. Like the nest he had disturbed only the other day – or was it week, or year perhaps; or was it tomorrow? Abie was easily confused about those things. He only knew he must avoid this nest of lovers as widely as the new captain's gun. Lovers did not appreciate small boys. Abie had been most shabbily treated by them. On that occasion it had been George's mother and the man who collected the rent and they had sworn at him and cuffed him and sent him away. Why, he could not tell. Certainly he was not disturbing their hunting, for they had no guns with them. They were just lying there and looking at each other. And when he had started to tell his mother about it she had said it was a nest of lovers and he was to avoid them. So he intended to do this and he would begin now.

Then there came a renewal of the sounds through the bracken and it was like a dog-fight under a blanket. Stifled, yet violent and agitated. There was a noise like something hitting something. Wood hitting wood perhaps. This was followed by a very wicked swear-word that was by no means stifled or under a blanket. Abie stopped and listened and the words he heard were destined to make him the envy of his class at kindergarten in the years to come.

'Right!' came a man's voice. 'Now you've asked for it!'

Abie made to crawl on, but his movement was arrested yet again by the sound of another shot, and this time he knew that the shots were flying through the bracken just above his head. The gun seemed to have nothing to do with what was taking place a few yards from him in the bracken, yet the two things were tied together by the afternoon and the pounding of the little boy's heart.

"Take that!' a woman's voice said. 'Take that, you brute!'

Abie ducked, but then he concluded she had not been talking to him. So he stepped boldly out.

The noise he made must have startled the woman, for there came an intaking of breath and an odd sob or two and the next instant Abie could hear the thoughtless breaking down of bracken as somebody tore a way through regardless.

Soon after this little Abie found the man.

The man was lying on his back and Abie nearly stepped on him. A big man with a moustache and wavy hair. He was lying staring up at the sky and not moving. From his head came a trickle of blood. It flowed from a wound above one eye and it was slowly soaking his white collar. Abie stared down at him for a little while, expecting to be sworn at. Then he tucked the gun under his left arm and walked away, not troubling about his special steps, but only eager to get into the woods and home.

# Body in the Bracken

The new captain sat on the lowest bough of an oak tree, one short leg dangling one side and one dangling on the other. He gripped a point-two-two rifle in his arms and a pipe of unknown calibre between his teeth. A short, plump little man with a mop of black, wiry hair and a brown, creased, clean-shaven face. A nautical figure with the innocent eyes of a baby. A man to inspire protection in a woman, trust in a child, fear in a coward and apprehension in a man of business. A man who knew the world without having seen more than the results of it in riverside taverns – for the new captain was neither new nor, strictly speaking, a captain. The new captain was Mr Albert Wiles, retired lighterman of the Thames barges. He was not a charlatan or a pretender, either, for the title by which he was known in Sparrowswick was not self-sought. He had been made a captain by Mr Mark Douglas, property-owner, landlord and despoiler of things beautiful. Albert Wiles had been made a captain because Sparrowswick had to have one. There always had been a captain in one of the little bungalows and there always would be. Moreover, the bungalow set aside for men of the sea was a little ship from ship. It rocked on unsafe stilts amongst the waves of shrubbery and instead of windows it had portholes. What was more, it was called 'The Ship'. In such a bungalow it stood to reason there had to be a seafarer. A man come from the lonely, watery places of the world. A wanderer. A bringer of salt and flapping canvas; a captain.

So it was only natural that when Albert Wiles had answered the advertisement regarding the tenancy of a bungalow on Sparrowswick Heath, wearing a rugged, peaked cap and smelling of deep water, Mr Mark Douglas had immediately mentally pigeon-holed him into the captain's bungalow. And it was only natural that since the previous captain – also a man of dubious rank – had obeyed a second-childhood urge and run back to sea, Captain Wiles should be called the new captain by all the people of the estate.

Captain Wiles then, sat on the lowermost bough of an oak tree on Sparrowswick Heath in the hot afternoon sunshine. He sat puffing at his pipe, perspiring and looking for rabbits. He was not a good huntsman in the true sense of the word, for although he had a good aim and had killed more rats than anyone else between Battersea and Woolwich, he was not at all certain what a live rabbit looked like. Nor what a pheasant looked like, or a hare. The only game with which he was acquainted hung on hooks around the front of The Fisheries near the Blackwall Tunnel, and to imagine those stiff, stuffy-looking objects leaping around in this strange and wonderful land was almost impossible. Nevertheless, Captain Wiles had taken three shots at moving objects that *might* have been rabbits or pheasants or something; and soon he was going to wander amongst the bracken and look for the results.

Meanwhile, it was pleasant to sit and watch and wait. It was pleasant to listen to the drone of bees amongst the heather, and the cheep of some bird above his head that sounded as though it had finished its dinner and was scraping a fork against an empty plate. It was pleasant to be alive in such a wild, rugged, yet cosy world. Pleasant to have it to yourself. The bungalow was quiet enough, but up here you were above quietness. Up here you were knocking on the pearly gates and hoping they wouldn't hear you. Captain Wiles let his eyes scan the tops of the bracken and he nodded, satisfied that he had that part of the heath to himself.

The captain had not forgotten the first time he went shooting. That had been a few days after he had moved in. He had come up here amongst the bracken and shot at what he had supposed to be a walking pheasant. But it had turned out to be a crawling Freddy Grayson. Mr Grayson had come to him that evening with a holed cap in his hand and wrath in his eye. He had told Captain Wiles a few things about dangerous shooting that he didn't know. He had told Captain Wiles a great many things blunt and to the point, finishing up with some advice about sticking to a pair of oars. The captain had vowed that never again would he go shooting amongst small boys. And so he was glad that, on this afternoon, the heath was deserted.

At last, long after the echoes of the last shot had gone over the hills, Captain Wiles swung himself agilely from the branch to the ground. He dusted the bark rust from his flannel trousers and set out along the path to inspect his killings.

The first thing he found was a white paper bag with a sticky aniseed ball in one corner and a neat point-two-two hole in the other.

He grunted and walked on.

He recollected that his second shot had been at something that moved near a big clump of broom. In his mind he had an exact photograph of where the moving object had been and where his shot had gone. Sure enough, in the exact spot, half-hidden by the gorse, he found a warm but dead hedgehog. Snuffling against the hedgehog were two baby hedgehogs. Two small, brown, prickly things too young to see clearly and making tiny squeaking noises like real babies.

The captain stood looking down at them. His brown face was touched with dismay. His heart, which had gloated over the death of a multitude of rats, wept for this dead mother, for these orphan children. For a moment he looked at the gun he carried, in a manner which made its destruction seem eminent. But then he sighed and passed on to the site of his third target.

Once again his sharp, innocent eyes led him straight to the spot. And this time his findings left him weak and shaken. He staggered back against a young ash tree that bent under his weight.

'Great Gordon Bennett!'

The dead man lay just as young Abie had seen him. The face, the moustache, the wavy hair, the blood. Everything.

'Christ Almighty!' said Captain Wiles. 'I've done him in!'

He looked frantically around him and all he could see were the trees. And from every tree dangled a noosed rope. Every tree, even to the furthest horizon, had become a gallows in his eyes. His mother had always said he would hang sooner or later, and it was later. Just as he had got through his life nicely. Just when he was looking forward to a quiet retirement. The times he had kept his temper and avoided brawls! The hundreds of times he had wanted to kill Tiger Wray – and had desisted simply because of wanting to live to prove his mother wrong and to enjoy the simplicity of the English countryside. And now this.... A harmless pot at a rabbit and he was a murderer. A killer. He groaned. It wasn't a bad shot, but by cripes! he'd done it now. He was in for it. 'What the hell was you doing laying here?' the captain asked the corpse. He groaned again.

He felt for the pulse of the dead man, more as a last politeness than anything. Then he ran his fingers through the pockets. He found an empty envelope addressed to 'Mr Harry Worp, Eighty-seven, Eastfield, Fulham'.

'Well,' said the captain philosophically, 'you're a long way from home, cock. And you'll never get back. Phone the police, Albert.' This last remark was addressed to himself. Having heard it, he got to his feet and began to walk

14

towards the woods and home. But even as he walked his mind was searching for an easy way out and he found it.

He stopped walking suddenly and turned to survey the glorious vista of greenery. He could barely see above the bracken and it all seemed more of a jungle to him than it would have done to a taller man.

'All this jungle,' he said, 'and one little body . . .'

He retraced his footsteps and stood a moment looking down at the corpse. The man was large, but the grass was silky through long drought. The captain regarded the shrubbery in the vicinity, looking for a place that would hide a body, not only in the lushness of summer but also in the barrenness of winter. Soon he spied an immense rhododendron bush that lifted its next year's flower-buds high into the sky and spread its evergreen skirts all round.

Without further hesitation he stooped, picked up the dead man's ankles like the shafts of a wheelbarrow, and with his stocky body straining forward he commenced the journey down the path between the bracken, towards the rhododendron that was to serve as a tomb for all time.

# Accessory After the Fact

Before Captain Wiles had got half-way to the rhododendron bush with his burden a woman appeared suddenly and miraculously in the middle of the path ahead. The little man, struggling along with short arms stretched behind him, his short legs shooting out beneath and his grim face tucked down into his collar, did not see his audience until his head was in danger of butting her in the stomach.

'Captain Wiles!' said the woman.

The captain dropped the dead man's ankles and stood to attention. At that moment Captain Wiles was not entirely himself. He stood looking into the woman's face and allowing perspiration to run unheeded down his nose, even though it tickled.

'Yes, ma'am,' he said.

The lady looked down at the body. She then looked at the captain's gun, which he had somehow managed to tuck into the top of his trousers. She said: 'Been shooting?'

The conversation having started, the captain's nerves loosened off a notch or two. He made the gun a little more comfortable in his trousers and wiped the sweat from his face with the back of his hand. He looked down at the body as though it was something with which he had experienced some difficulty.

'Yes,' he said. 'Bit of an accident. He's dead.'

The lady touched the body gingerly and a little distastefully with the toe of her shoe. 'Yes, isn't he?' she remarked.

The captain licked his lips. Exactly what to say next he did not know. This, then, was Miss Graveley. A lady he had seen only from a distance. A lady whom everyone, certainly every man, saw only from a distance. A reserved lady. A middle-aged man-hater. A spinster by choice and inclination. Miss Graveley of 'The Haven', which stood behind hollyhocks next to 'The Ship'. Miss Graveley, whom Mr Douglas had described as a confirmed virgin.

'Do you know him, ma'am?' the captain asked apprehensively.

She shook her head. She studied the face of the corpse as it lay on the soft grass. 'What are you going to do with him, Captain?' she asked. She spoke as though the body were a trophy and she was expecting the captain to put it into a glass case.

Captain Wiles took his fears and flung them into the bracken. 'Hide him. Cover him up. Forget him,' he rasped hoarsely.

Miss Graveley seemed to consider this for a moment and the captain watched her face for her response, as a small boy might watch his school-teacher before some important announcement regarding half-holidays. At last the lady said: 'Don't you think you should inform the police, Captain?'

'No!' Captain Wiles was definite. Suddenly the trees around them dropped their hanging nooses again. The little captain clutched Miss Graveley's arm. 'Forget you saw me, ma'am! Forget all about it, for God's sake! It was an accident. An accident. He was laying in the bracken. How was I to know? He couldn't have been up to no good. Don't say nothing, ma'am.'

A faint smile came into the lady's face as the captain worked himself into a state of terror. She removed his hand and stepped away. 'Do as you think best, Captain. I'm sure you must have met many similar situations in your travels in foreign lands. I certainly won't say anything. It was most unfortunate.'

The captain regained his composure and broadened his

chest. 'I've seen worse things happen,' he admitted. 'Much worse things. I remember when I was in Orinoco –'

'Hadn't you better . . . er . . . remove this . . . er . . .?'

Captain Wiles spat on his hands and took up the dead man's ankles again. 'You're right, ma'am. Y'know something? I'm glad I met you. I feel better for telling somebody. Funny, eh?'

'I'm glad I've helped you,' said Miss Graveley. 'Perhaps you would care to come over for a cup of tea later on?'

The captain blinked. She wasn't a bad sort at all. Attractive too, in a way. Nice grey eyes, plenty of dark hair . . .

'Yes, I'd like a spot of char,' he said. 'What time?'

'Five o'clock?'

'Okey doke,' said the captain. He began to drag the body off down the path. 'You better get along now. Don't want to be an accessory after the fact.'

'Good-bye then, Captain Wiles.'

'Ta-ta,' said the captain, digging his toes in.

# Let's Run Home and Eat Cakes!

After Miss Graveley had gone and just as the captain had reached the rhododendron, he heard the shouting of a small boy. The captain looked over his shoulder and was horrified to see the top of a woman's head just appearing above the bracken at a bend in the path he had traversed. There was no time to get the body into the bush so the captain did what was next best and hid his own body under the rhododendron. Immediately he heard a triumphant cry, followed by the thud of running feet.

'Don't touch it!' came a faint and feminine voice. 'Don't touch it, Abie!'

'No, Mummy,' said a breathless Abie, arriving panting by the corpse, his small gun held at the ready.

The captain lay on his stomach peering from under the thick foliage. He cursed his bad luck. All afternoon he had been alone and now he wanted to be alone the place was crowded with unnecessary people.

'I *said* follow the blood!' exclaimed Abie delightedly, as his mother came up. 'I *said* follow the blood, didn't I?'

Abie's mother grimaced at the sight of the bloody face. Then suddenly she exclaimed: 'My God! Harry!'

The heart of Captain Wiles turned to a heavy grade of commercial lead. The chance of keeping the body privately and decently hidden now was nil. She knew it. It had a name. It was called Harry. Probably she could remember when it talked and walked and breathed and filled in football coupons. Certainly she would never agree, as Miss

Graveley had done so readily, to hiding it under the rhododendron for all eternity. And in any case the little boy would talk. No, he might as well make a clean breast of it. The captain ran his finger around his neck.

'Harry!' breathed the young woman again, kneeling down and looking into the dead face. 'Thank God!'

Now those two simple words caused the little captain some astonishment. He peered very hard indeed into the young woman's face and he read there no grief. Indeed, she was smiling, as though half-expecting the corpse to enjoy the secret joke.

'The last of Harry,' she said.

'Who is it, Mummy?' said the little boy.

'Don't you remember?' the woman said, bringing him closer to obtain a better view. 'Can't you remember, Abie?'

The little boy studied the face carefully, then shook his head. 'What's he laying there for?' he asked.

'He's asleep,' said Abie's mother. 'He's in a deep sleep. A wonderful deep sleep.'

'How did he hurt his head?' said the little boy.

'Putting it where it wasn't wanted I should think,' said the mother happily.

'Will he get better?'

The young woman stood up. In the sunlight she looked beautiful. In any light she would have looked beautiful. The captain felt glad he had killed Harry if it brought such joy and happiness and beauty to this young woman. The captain's heart danced with joy just looking at her. A wonderful, happy young thing in the sunshine of a wonderful, happy day. A wonderful, happy boy and a wonderful, happy world. The captain felt wonderfully happy lying on his podgy belly with his brown face resting on his hands and his innocent baby eyes resting on the beautiful young woman.

'I don't think he will get better,' said the young mother

joyously. She took her son's hand. 'Come on, Abie, let's run home and eat cakes!'

As they ran away to eat cakes, leaving the dead man staring into the chalk-blue sky, Captain Wiles began to ease himself out from under the bush. The gun, which was still stuck in his trousers, was digging uncomfortably into his thigh. He began to form a glowing and friendly feeling for the people who lived in the bungalows of Sparrowswick. His neighbours. His first impression, gathered from Mr Grayson, the father of the boy whose cap he had damaged, was erroneous. Mr Grayson was obviously not representative of Sparrowswick. It was easy to see that Abie's mother would not care *where* he put the body; the little boy would forget – and anyway he was too young to understand death – and Miss Graveley would not tell. Miss Graveley was going to make tea for him. Miss Graveley approved of him. Him, of all men.

As the captain drew himself out from the bush a man dashed up the path. The captain withdrew quickly into the rhododendron bush. But he felt certain he had been seen.

The man came running. He was a tall, thin man, wearing tropical white ducks and an ancient white panama. His face was thin to the point of starvation and his eyes, behind a pair of spectacles, were large and eager. He did not see the captain because he was chasing a butterfly. He was chasing a large and rare and magnificent butterfly with a large and rare and magnificent net. He saw neither the captain nor the body and consequently he tripped over the body and fell headlong, pushing his net right under the rhododendron and within half an inch of the captain's nose.

Slowly and broken-heartedly the tall, thin man got to his spindly legs. Without looking at the body he began to search his very limited horizon for a sign of the butterfly. It was obvious to the watching captain that unless the corpse suddenly sprouted coloured wings it hadn't the faintest chance of discovery. Suddenly the butterfly, having waited sportingly for the chaser to regain his feet, fluttered into the air from a leaf of the rhododendron bush and in a split second the thin man and the butterfly were off over the heath again, the butterfly gaily leading.

The captain rested his face sideways on his hands for a moment to still his beating heart and recover his breath. It was indeed his lucky day.

''Struth!'' he remarked.

# The Man and the Blonde

The afternoon grew older and warmer. The bracken, the acres of bracken, the many level stretches and valleys and rises of bracken, supported a shivering haze of heat. A shivering, quivering, dizzy haze of reflected warmth. The bracken, the deep, shiny rhododendron, the chestnuts, the heather and the soft, fine grass and all the heath breathed a warm, visible breath. The afternoon grew old and warm and mature.

Captain Albert Wiles grew tired and hot and sticky. Usually by this time he was asleep and snoring. Already, his breathing had changed to yawning. The corpse lying unattended on the broad, sunlit path grew stiff and attracted flies. The captain decided to get rid of this body once and for all.

He was crawling out of the shrub with this objective when there came a crashing and a crackling in the undergrowth. With a sigh – a patient and resigned sigh – the captain wriggled backwards into his hiding-place.

He had scarce settled himself, his face on his hands, his rump high, his knees tucked under him, when a tramp walked round the bush and stood staring down at the corpse. He was a very English and very dirty tramp. A tramp redolent of many doss-houses and haystacks. A tramp touched in some subtle manner by all the counties of England. The reeds of the Fen country thatched his head; his face was the brown and grey clay of the Black Country; his dirt-ringed eyes held the muddy water of the Upper Thames; his jacket was a remnant from a night at 'The Dorchester' – somebody else's night – while his trousers were woven and unwoven with the straw of the Cotswolds. He was the complete tramp – at least, he was almost the complete tramp. He had everything the successful tramp should have except a pair of boots. His feet were naked except for the layers of dirt.

For a moment he stood staring down at the body. He touched it with his foot. He bent over it and spat into its staring eye. No living eye could have suffered that unblinking, so the tramp was satisfied. And being satisfied he sat down alongside the corpse and began unlacing its shoes.

All this Captain Wiles watched and as the sight of the happy young mother had made him glad to be a murderer, so the sight of this dirty, impersonal predatory man-tramp made him regret his irresponsible shooting. The captain closed his eyes for a moment and for the first time sent up a prayer for forgiveness. He vowed he would never go shooting again. He vowed that if he escaped the noose just this once he would turn Evangelist or join the Salvation Army.

While the captain was praying and the tramp was taking the dead man's shoes and socks, a man and woman came walking along one of the many tributaries of the main path. A man and woman holding hands. A couple. They walked in a nervous fashion, as though half afraid of being seen. It was obvious they were married, but married to different people.

The woman was a blonde. The woman was, moreover, A Blonde. One of the stereotyped blondes. A blonde with high curls of hard gold. A blonde with blue, toneless eyes. A blonde with one of the six shades of lipstick applied in one of the six ways. She was a blonde out of a moulding, mass-produced by the age, thrown out by the million, conceived by progress, born of cinema out of magazine. She was one of the nameless, ageless women of the twentieth century. Nothing she had was her own; nothing *of* her *was* her. She was the blonde of Piccadilly, High Street, Market Street and the council houses. The blonde of young men's dull moments and old men's bright moments. The blonde you meet in every town, village and hedgerow in the world. Her toilet requirements, her underclothes and the way she said 'maybe' were a mutual property.

This international institution walked Sparrowswick with her landlord, Mark Douglas, for it was rent day.

Mark Douglas was a lover of blondes. He was also a lover of brunettes, red-heads, albinos, negresses, Mulattoes, Eurasians, Asiatics and hotel receptionists. Mark Douglas loved anything in skirts that didn't play bagpipes. He was a small man, full of an unpleasant energy.

They were laughing and talking as they walked, even though they were keeping their eyes alert. Every time they laughed Mark Douglas took the opportunity to slap the blonde's behind. This seemed to give them both a lot of pleasure.

'Last night,' said the blonde, 'he asked me how I got bitten in such queer places.'

They roared with laughter and Mark Douglas smacked her.

'Where were the queer places?' he asked.

They roared with laughter and he smacked her again.

'Where do *you* think!' said the blonde.

They roared with laughter and he smacked her again.

'What kind of bites – man or beast?' he asked.

They roared with laughter and he smacked her again.

'Mosquitoes!' she said, and the word was on the bubble of her last outburst of laughter.

He smacked her again and this time he kept his hand on her. 'Where shall we sit down?' he asked, conveying the importance of his words with his fingers.

'I don't think we ought,' said the blonde, using the blonde vocabulary.

'There's a big rhododendron over there,' said the little landlord.

He guided her towards the big rhododendron. When they

came out on to the main path by the shrub the tramp had just completed the transfer of the shoes and socks. As soon as the couple made their appearance he had the good sense to lie back with the corpse and stare into the sky.

'Tramps!' said the blonde, disgusted.

'Lying right across the path!' said Mark Douglas.

'We'll carry on a bit up that other path,' said the blonde.

'You're telling me!' said Mark Douglas, slapping her again and moulding her with his fingers towards another secondary path in the bracken.

Presently, while Captain Wiles was falling asleep under the rhododendron, the tramp got up and walked away, muttering to himself about the relief of Mafeking.

# Wiggs' Emporium

While these momentous things were happening on the heath, nothing was going on down amongst the trees and the bungalows. Nothing was happening, the way it happened every afternoon when the people who came home to lunch had gone back and the tradesmen had finished calling. It was an active, participative kind of nothing.

Butterflies flew in little couplets amongst the bushes and into the gardens. White butterflies and brown, the small, valueless kind. Butterflies and cherry-eaters. Bees swam around the heads of gladioli, stopping to kiss and sample and then swimming on, fatuously, contentedly. Wasps settled like buzzards on fallen fruit and dustbins, while double hollyhocks stood in groups catching the breeze and talking things over.

So far as the world was concerned – the world which came along the road in motor-cars and buses and cycles – the Sparrowswick Bungalow Estate was a thick wood which clung to the side of a hill, with here and there a roof or a chimney showing amongst the leaves. The entrance to the estate was a stony track with a bungalow on one side and an old, ivy-covered cottage on the other. This stony track was just wide enough to take a medium-sized motor-car. Higher up, out of sight of the road, other tracks dribbled away between the trees and these were just wide enough to take a small motor-car or a motor-cycle combination. From these paths other little paths of dirt and leaf-mould wandered away to isolated bungalows in which lived, of necessity, people with feet or bicycles.

In the old ivy-covered cottage by the road lived the widow Wiggs, proprietress of the Wiggs' Emporium. Mrs Wiggs sold groceries, lisle stockings, bacon and other provisions, toothache tincture on cards, beautifully coloured packets of seeds, stationery, shopping-bags and everything imaginable except the thing you wanted when it was early closing in the nearest town. Mrs Wiggs also sold original paintings, water-colours, oils, black-and-white sketches, half-tones; all with the artist's name inscribed off-handedly yet unmistakably in one corner: Sam Marlow.

Besides these examples of painting and drawing the widow Wiggs sold other forms of fine art. At least, she stocked other forms. She stocked little wisps of poetry written in fine Indian ink on white cards. She stocked flowers and ornaments fashioned from coloured wax and dull with the dust of months. She stocked little books bound in hand-patterned leather which could be used for contract bridge scoring or as a diary. And by some amazing feat of packing Mrs Wiggs stocked all these commodities in her front room, which was roughly two yards square and contained as well as a small bacon-slicing machine with a broken blade, a short counter and a brass till. In this small front room turned into a shop then, were stocked groceries, lisle stockings, bacon and other provisions, toothache tincture on cards, beautifully coloured packets of seeds, stationery, shopping-bags and fine art. All this plus the fixtures; one bacon-slicing machine, one till and one Mrs Wiggs. By careful manoeuvring it was also possible to get two customers in the shop, though it meant one had to be small and sit on a biscuit tin.

The window of this shop was one pane wide, half being taken up with feminine and intimate drapery, and the other half with a painting of a glossy-haired young man advertising cigarettes.

The history of the Wiggs' was the history of success. The old cottage had stood there long before the bungalows were dreamed of; long before the ancestors of Mark Douglas had begun to disclaim him as a descendant. The cottage had been a game-warden's cottage and Henry Wiggs had been a game-warden. It follows that Milly Wiggs had been a game-warden's wife.

When the landed gentry to whom the shooting estate belonged became buried gentry, it was found necessary to sell the estate to meet the legacy of debts. It was then that Mark Douglas, would-be landlord and lover of blondes, conceived his plan.

He had bought all the land except the piece on which the cottage stood. This had been left, freehold, to the Wiggs' in appreciation of the game they had preserved for killing. Henry Wiggs, a shrewd man who could see one hundred and fifty paces on a dark night, had immediately gone into business. By the time the estate was built – a six-week miracle – he had stocked in his front room all that human beings living in a wood might need. In the years that followed a brisk trade was carried on in the little cottage, for the nearest shopping centre was three miles away – a garden city which sprawled across a neighbouring hill like the dirty red wounds of a gravel workings.

Sixpences passed across the counter by the thousand. Sixpences and shillings and, after the drapery had started, odd sums ending in three-farthings. Confidences, too, were exchanged across this counter and gossip was rampant. The little store became to Sparrowswick Estate what the centre of any busy metropolis is to any busy metropolis. The Wiggs came to know the new woodland denizens as well as they had done the old quadrupeds and to like and dislike and recognize the foxes and the rabbits and the snakes amongst them. The people with no money began to run up their little bills and pay them, while the people with plenty of money began to run up big bills and leave them unpaid, and gradually a state of urban normality came to the heath.

The death of Henry Wiggs could be directly attributed to

the unpleasant Mr Douglas. One autumn evening, on his way to collect some rent from one of his blonde tenants, he had called in on Henry Wiggs and asked that ex-gamekeeper if he stocked a certain commodity. Mr Wiggs had been sharpening the bacon slicer at the time and he had almost cut off the top of his finger. He made a noise similar to a hog in distress, which Mr Mark Douglas had interpreted as 'No'. Thereupon Mr Douglas had suggested, well-meaningly, that Mr Wiggs would do well to keep a little supply in some discreet corner of the shop. Moreover, Mr Douglas had personally guaranteed a steady sale of this commodity. It was at this stage that Mr Henry Wiggs had dashed into his back parlour and appeared a moment later grasping the double-barrelled shotgun.

There had then occurred a chase the like of which had never been seen before on that heath or any other. Mark Douglas had gone running wildly away up through the woods on to the heath with Henry Wiggs in hot pursuit. And after Henry there came Mrs Wiggs, and after Mrs Wiggs the blonde with whom Mr Douglas had an appointment, and after her most of the residents of the estate, for it was a time of day when a little diversion is welcome. All over the heath they had travelled at a smart pace, and four times the barrels of the shot-gun were discharged without effect. Nobody knew the exact reason for the pursuit of their landlord by their provisioner, but it was naturally assumed that Mr Wiggs had found Mr Douglas in a compromising situation with Mrs Wiggs, for although Mrs Wiggs was plain and elderly she did wear a skirt and she did not play bagpipes.

Eventually, by hiding all night in the bracken, Mark Douglas had escaped the wrath of Mr Wiggs. But Henry never fully recovered from that chase. He was no young man and the landlord had shown a turn of speed and ingenuity that no pheasant or hare of Henry's experience had ever shown. Henry strained his heart. He was on his death-bed for six months, but never once did he regret his action, for right to the end his shop retained a Catholic purity of stock.

# People With Hats On

Such was the background of the Wiggs' Emporium, standing that hot, summer afternoon between the world and the woods; between Sparrowswick and 'The Rest'.

Mrs Wiggs attended her stall. The stall was a number of planks thrown across trestles and covered by a white oil-cloth. This stall stood half a dozen yards in front of the cottage and almost on the verge of the road. It was a stall designed to stop motorists and other road-users. There was still-lemonade on this stall and cut flowers and sandwiches and aspirins. Some of the brighter water-colours signed 'Sam Marlow' leaned against the front and above them the wisps of poetry, threaded by their corners with darning-wool, hung from drawing-pins.

This was Mrs Wiggs' summer enterprise. This was a way of capturing trade other than her staple trade. Once, on a Thursday, a charabanc had stopped at this stall and she had sold all her still-lemonade and a bunch of asters. Somebody had talked of buying one of the pictures, but it had come to nothing. Ever after that Mrs Wiggs watched the road for charabancs but never did she see another. It was to be supposed that that particular charabanc had wandered from its route.

Mrs Wiggs, then, sat in the shade of a chestnut tree, behind her stall, and waited for trade. She was a narrow woman with a broad, accommodating mind. Narrow shoulders and hips and a narrow mouth. She had no colour, either florid or pale. She was a neutral woman, with nothing positive or negative about her. She was so insignificant that even if you saw her many times in a single day you would find it hard, under close examination, to swear that you had seen her at all. Yet she was a kindly woman and tolerant, thoroughly agreeing with everybody.

Suddenly, yet gradually, to this woman came a song. Amidst the occasional traffic noises, the straining of lorries over the hill, the changing of gears going down the hill, the whirr of faulty crown wheels, the rhythmic flip of asymmetrical tyres, above and through all these noises came a song. A strong, virile, baritone voice floating high above the trees behind her singing the song 'Jerusalem':

> 'And did those feet in ancient time
> Walk upon England's mountains green . . .'

A song that swelled into the sunshine and became a part of the strong, hot light. A song that might well have come with the sunshine as one of Heaven's odd amenities.

As she heard the song she sighed a little and reached over to set the paintings to better advantage. She looked at the paintings and in them she could recognize the voice she was hearing. It had the same confident, carefree style. The same ethereal yet earthy style. It was the same man. It was Sam Marlow.

> 'Bring me my bow of burning gold . . .'

Down through the trees and the shrubs came the voice. Down past 'The Ship' and 'The Haven' and 'Bon Vista' and 'Chaos' and 'The Chestnuts' and 'The Woodlands' and all the bungalow names in the world. Down through the woods and up over the heath went the voice. Swelling into the limitless spaces of the summer sky. All heard it save one and he was dead. All heard it and in some way were gladdened by it. Abie's mother, in the garden of 'Chaos', heard it as she was feeding cakes to her son and she watched the wonderful figure striding down through the foliage. Miss Graveley heard it as she was combing her hair and smiling to herself in a mirror in 'The Haven'. In Miss Graveley, who had heard that voice so many times and remained unmoved, it wrought painful, ecstatic emotions. As the young god went past she covered her face with her hands and cried for joy. Up on the heath a tramp heard it. This tramp, comfortably shod, was walking between the heat-soaked bracken and his thoughts were concerned with the solution of triangles according to the ancient Greeks. This song immediately sent his mind along fresh tracks towards the migration of the Asiatics into the American continent. In the bracken Mark Douglas, the landlord, heard it and immediately slapped the behind of George's blonde mother, at which she giggled. And in his dreams beneath the rhododendron the new captain heard it and he smiled, and by some curious reflex action his snores subsided.

Only the corpse of the man called Harry was untouched by this glorious song on this glorious day in this glorious country. It lay, shoeless and sockless, staring bleakly into the chalk-blue sky.

Down through the bushes towards the road went Sam Marlow the artist. A young man, carved it seemed from solid gold. He was a big young man. He wore clothes, but they were more a convention than a covering. Indeed, there was much of him uncovered. A broad, thick body, well-proportioned yet not muscular. The crown of his head swayed about six feet above the ground when he walked. His thin hair was sparse and fair from sun bleaching. His eyes were blue if you could see them, but usually they were screwed up as though viewing a distant sunset. He had a full mouth of white teeth and a square, stubbly chin. His throat was long and prominent and his chest, a golden barrel, made his ragged shirt look silly and inadequate. His waist was not athletic, being as far round as his legs were long. His old flannel trousers gaped at the top as he walked and his navel was plainly and unashamedly visible amongst his torn shirt and a quantity of hair. He wore sandals and no socks and his feet were big and chocolate brown. He looked as he sounded, as though he were bursting with summer.

Under his arm he carried a large water-colour.

He reached Mrs Wiggs and her stall with his song still unfinished. Reluctant to stop singing, being intoxicated with the words and his own voice, he walked around her three times before coming to the last fine note. The thin, colourless and elderly woman stared out across the road and the field and woods beyond, enjoying the music but passing no comment. When he had finished she said: 'Good afternoon, Mr Marlow.'

He looked at the stall. He walked from end to end looking at his pictures. When he had walked along the stall one way he turned and walked back. At last he stood in front of Mrs Wiggs, the new painting held between his stomach and his toes.

'Woman! Woman! You haven't sold a picture!' He swept his hand in a grand gesture of disgust. 'All my pictures standing in the same place!'

The woman was unruffled. She shrugged apologetically. 'There's so few cars. . . . They don't seem to want . . . I think the lemonade takes their attention . . .'

'You naughty, naughty Wiggy!' cried the artist, waving his fist at her. 'You naughty, naughty Wiggy! The lemonade indeed! Throw it away. Drink it.' His voice descended to the soft register of pathos and he bowed his head. 'Not a picture sold . . .'

'I'm sorry, Mr Marlow. Let's see your new one. Hold it up.'

'I've a mind *not* to let you see it,' he said. 'You don't deserve to see it. How am I going to eat?' He thumped his stomach and the woman tried not to look at his navel.

'Mr Wiggs always said it's a funny spot for anything like that,' said Mrs Wiggs.

Sam Marlow turned about with a suddenness that made the woman flinch. He took a long look at the empty fields and the woods. He could see two cows, a crow, and the smoke from a distant train. He turned back to the woman as though struck by a sudden thought. He put his face down to hers.

'You think we'd do better in Bond Street?'

Mrs Wiggs looked uncertain. 'If there's more people there, Mr Marlow.'

'Oh, there are! There is! Crowds. Thousands of people. Millions and billions of people.'

'It might be better then,' said Mrs Wiggs mildly.

'But!' the young artist exclaimed. 'But!'

Their faces were very close together now and Mrs Wiggs was waiting patiently for the disadvantages.

'What *kind* of people?' he said. 'What sort? What *breed*? Stop! I'll tell you, Wiggy. They're *little* people, Wiggy . . .' He crouched down in a demonstration and he screwed his face up and looked like a squat scarecrow. '*Little* people!' he hissed. '*People with hats on!*'

Mrs Wiggs nodded, understandingly. Sam straightened up and scratched his chest.

'What are your cheapest cigarettes?' he asked rationally, his voice twenty decibels lower.

'Woodbines, Mr Marlow, same as always.'

'What's the smallest quantity you have?'

'Packets of five, Mr Marlow.'

'Give me five, Wiggy, and the scissors.'

'Yes, Mr Marlow.'

Mrs Wiggs gave him a packet of five cigarettes and the scissors she used for trimming the flower-stalks. She sat and watched him cut the cigarettes in half and tuck them back into the packet. He then held up his new painting.

'Oh, Mr Marlow!' she exclaimed.

'You like it?'

'It's wonderful!'

He sighed with gratification.

She said: 'What is it?'

He sighed a resigned sigh. 'Good old Wiggy,' he said, putting the painting alongside the others. 'My sternest critic.'

Mrs Wigg accepted the compliment gravely. 'I think your work is beautiful. So does Mrs Rogers.'

'Aha!' exclaimed the artist, his voice expanding again. 'So you talk about me?'

Mrs Wiggs was slightly embarrassed. 'Well, I only said . . .'

'That's the pretty woman with the little boy at "Chaos"?'

'Yes, Mr Marlow.'

'And what does the pretty little thing think of me, eh?'

'Well . . .' Mrs Wiggs suffered the natural reluctance of a confidence breaker. 'She thinks you ought to be on the stage.'

Sam Marlow took this as a boxer might take a heavy blow. He shook his head and recovered. 'Let's go into the Emporium,' he suggested quietly. 'I want some food.'

Mrs Wiggs and the artist walked away from the stall and into the shop as a big and impressive Rolls-Royce car slunk to a stop against the pictures and a man wearing a sun helmet and horn-rimmed spectacles looked at the pictures and waited for attention.

# A Piece of Coloured Ribbon

While Mrs Wiggs was shaving off a quarter of streaky from a piece of flank at sixpence a pound, Miss Graveley came in. Sam Marlow gallantly stood on the biscuit tin to allow her room. He looked at Miss Graveley with interest, for she seemed in a state of agitation. There was an excitement about her that his artistic eye was quick to notice. They had lived on the Sparrowswick slopes for years, ever since she had retired with a small annuity from her Uncle Moses and he had been sent down from Cambridge with a minute allowance from his father. They had lived on this bosky hill for years, passed each other scores of times, tripped over each other many times and yet never spoken, nor did they know each other's names.

But on this occasion Miss Graveley did speak. She said: 'What a wonderful afternoon!'

Sam said: 'So was yesterday, but you didn't say anything to *me* about it.'

Mrs Wiggs said: 'It's a regular heat wave.'

Outside in the road the Rolls-Royce sounded a deep and musical electric hooter.

'Those marvellous paintings,' said Miss Graveley, smiling at Sam. 'Somebody told me they were yours – why don't you sell them and make a lot of money? Think how pleasant it would be.'

Sam regarded her as though she had really hit on something. 'I must think about it,' he said.

'And that song,' said Miss Graveley. 'How well you sing it!'

'What do you want to borrow?' Sam asked.

Miss Graveley threw up her pale hands. 'Oh, dear, no! I do think we need a little encouragement sometimes, though, don't you, Mr Marlow?'

'How do you know my name?' asked Sam.

'It's on the pictures, isn't it?'

'It's not supposed to be readable,' Sam said.

'You can tell it's not supposed to be,' said Miss Graveley. 'They're all very professional, don't you think, Mrs Wiggs?'

'I do indeed, Miss Graveley,' said Mrs Wiggs, wrapping up the scrap of bacon. 'I was only saying the other day –'

'Thank you for your encouragement, Miss Graveley,' Sam said generously.

'Now I wonder how you know *my* name,' said Miss Graveley, with the air of a kitten.

'Wiggy just told me,' Sam said.

'Wiggy? Oh – Mrs Wiggs? I say, what a topping little nickname. Do let me call you Wiggy, Mrs Wiggs.'

'It's a pleasure, I'm sure,' said Mrs Wiggs. 'Here you are, Mr Marlow – bacon, margarine, sugar, tea, baked beans, potatoes, half a cabbage and some salt – it comes to one and fourpence. Oh, and the cigarettes. It comes to one and sixpence altogether.'

'*Does* it,' said Sam Marlow, feeling deeply in his shabby pockets. He wriggled his hands down to the furthermost recesses of his trouser pockets then, since he was wearing no jacket, he made a business of feeling in his hip pocket. The space in the shop was so limited that his gyrations sent two biscuit tins crashing to the floor and the big painting of the glossy-haired young man in the window leaned forward as though suddenly interested in the flower border directly under the window.

'Perhaps you'd better go outside and look,' said Mrs Wiggs, 'while I serve Miss Graveley.'

Sam Marlow the artist went out on to the sunlit front

space and searched for one and sixpence. As soon as he appeared the man in the Rolls-Royce played a wonderful *arpeggio* on his electric hooters. Sam looked across at him and waved. The man was sitting on the near side of the car and he was so taken with the pictures lining the stall that he was almost out of the car.

Pretty soon Sam came back into the shop with one shilling and twopence in his hand.

'I've got one and twopence,' he said.

'Just a minute, Mr Marlow,' Mrs Wiggs said.

It was then Sam became aware of something important happening. Miss Graveley was standing holding up a large, thick tea-cup to the light. It was a big, cheap cup, though not chipped; but the middle-aged spinster was holding it and treating it as though it were some fine and ancient porcelain.

'One and twopence –' Sam began again.

'Pssssh!' said Mrs Wiggs.

Sam succumbed to the tension. He studied the cup over Miss Graveley's shoulder. She turned and stared at him. Her face was serious and pale with the labour of her deciding. When she spoke she enunciated her words carefully, as a prime minister about to sell out the country might do.

'What do you think?' she said.

Sam pondered. 'I think it will hold tea,' he said.

'How about the size? What about the handle? Is it finger size?'

Sam put his finger through the handle. 'It's *my* finger size.'

Miss Graveley took hold of his hands and studied his fingers. Mrs Wiggs stood by her brass till awaiting a decision, her face expressionless. Miss Graveley swung around to her, animated by the importance of her decision.

'I'll take it!'

'Twopence-ha'penny,' said Mrs Wiggs, in her level tone.

'And the saucer?'

'Four-and-a-half all together,' said Mrs Wiggs.

While Mrs Wiggs wrapped up the cup and saucer, being careful to put soft paper inside the cup and between the cup and the saucer, Miss Graveley watched with a dream-like quality in her eyes. She caught sight of herself in a scrap of chromium plating on the bacon machine. She touched her hair, lifting it from her neck.

'I think I'll have some ribbon,' she announced.

'I want to get up on the heath to paint before the best of the sunlight goes,' Sam said reasonably. 'If you'd just take my one and twopence and put the odd fourpence on the slate –'

'Ribbon?' said Mrs Wiggs. She looked up at Miss Graveley and there was a perplexed expression in her insignificant face. Mrs Wiggs had come to expect certain things of certain people and Miss Graveley was buying out of character. She had bought a big, ugly cup and now she was talking about ribbon.

'What kind of ribbon?'

Miss Graveley studied her face and hair in the scrap of chromium. 'I think blue –' She turned suddenly to Sam. 'You're an artist, Mr Marlow. What colour ribbon shall I have?'

'Red's always a good colour,' Sam said, 'if it's for an Easter egg or a parcel of some kind.'

'It's for my hair,' said Miss Graveley.

Mrs Wiggs' bunion began to throb, which was a sign that things were getting a little beyond her. 'I think I've got a lemonade customer,' she said, catching the last notes from the Rolls-Royce again.

Sam took Miss Graveley by the arm. 'How can you talk of lemonade at a time like this?' He spoke to Mrs Wiggs over his shoulder. He then addressed Miss Graveley. 'You want some coloured ribbon for your hair?'

Miss Graveley nodded.

Sam's eyes rested for a moment on the wrapped cup and

saucer. 'Something special going to happen?' he hazarded.

Miss Graveley blushed and laid her eyelashes on her cheeks in a way she had not done for some twenty years. '*Somebody's coming to tea*,' she said.

'A man?'

Miss Graveley nodded, mutely.

'You old tease!' said Sam, in a congratulatory tone.

'Old!'

Mrs Wiggs peered out of the window and set the glossy-haired young man to rights. Outside, the man had got out of the Rolls-Royce and was looking more closely at the paintings.

'That was figurative,' said Sam gallantly.

'How old do you think I am, young man?' said Miss Graveley, a little apprehensively.

'Fifty-five,' said Sam. 'How old do *you* think you are?'

'Forty-two,' said Miss Graveley. 'I can show you my certificate.'

Sam looked at her and sighed. 'You'll have to show more than your certificate to prove that. You should have your hair cut. A nice bob.'

'I think I'll just go out and see what that gentleman wants,' said Mrs Wiggs.

'You stay here, Mrs Wiggs,' said Miss Graveley, digesting the artist's constructive remark. She once again looked at herself in the bacon machine. She could see herself now with a bob. She looked very beautiful. She leaned towards Mrs Wiggs. 'Could you bob my hair, Wiggy?'

Mrs Wiggs shuffled. 'I don't know, I'm sure,' she said.

'*I* know, I'm sure,' said Sam. 'Take her in the back parlour, Wiggy. I'll go and get the scissors from the stall.'

Mrs Wiggs dithered. 'Well, all right, Miss Graveley. Come through.'

Miss Graveley, with the air of a crusader, followed the proprietress of Wiggs' Emporium into the back parlour. Sam Marlow went to the stall outside. The man in the horn-rimmed glasses had just replaced a picture against the stall and was looking at his watch.

'I say . . .' he said, when he saw Sam.

Sam poured out a glass of lemonade and thrust it into the man's hand. He took the scissors up and strode back to the ivy-covered cottage.

The man began to follow him. Then he looked at his watch again, gulped the lemonade, and got back into his car. As Sam went in to cut off Miss Graveley's hair, the Rolls-Royce purred away.

# Let's Get This Straight

Sam Marlow, the artist, climbed the same woodland path that Abie, the small boy, had climbed some two hours earlier. Instead of a gun, however, under his arm he carried an easel and the things with which to make coloured pictures of what he saw and felt and believed. The woodland came to Sam as a series of separate pictures. He looked to the left and to the right; he looked up and down and sometimes he stopped and looked back the way he had come and saw the steep path framed by the trees with, right at the bottom, the front gate of the first bungalow.

He came out on to the heath and continued his slow walk. He walked as slowly and silently as little Abie had walked, and he might easily have been stalking big game instead of new angles.

Soon Sam Marlow came upon the dead hedgehog. There was a solitary bluebottle settled on the bullet wound and when Sam lunged his foot towards it the bluebottle leapt sideways after the manner of bluebottles and zoomed away into a wide spiral, its greedy, bulbous eyes still fixed on the blood it had left.

Sam turned the hedgehog over gently with his sandal. He heard a tiny commotion in the bracken nearby and he walked across and looked down intently. He saw the baby hedgehogs moving around and crying gently to each other. Sam was filled with a vast and overwhelming sorrow. He lay down his painting equipment and took the small creatures in his hands. He looked into their small, pointed faces and he rubbed their soft bellies with his forefinger. Pretty soon he had them wrapped in bracken and canvas while their mother lay beneath the leaf-mould under a gorse bush.

The bluebottle watched him, angrily buzzing around his head and making as if to attack, but Sam took no notice. When all was done and the babies had joined his pack of paints and brushes he turned as if to go. But before he actually moved he swung around with great violence and slapped the bluebottle into the ground in one vicious gesture, quickly stamping out its sickly life against the soft grass.

Sam moved on through the maze of paths, trying to think of a good song to sing. Through his head leapt 'The Invitation to the Waltz' and other wonderful tunes, but he let them remain there, for there were times when the singing in his head was more wondrous than anything to which he could give voice.

The body of the man called Harry came as a complete surprise to Sam Marlow, though not as a tragedy, as the hedgehog had been. He thought what a queer thing it was, on an afternoon like this, to find a man's body without shoes. First a dead hedgehog with two live babies, then a dead man with two bare feet. Surely here was a sign of some kind. Surely it all meant something. Sam felt strangely full. Mysterious emotions moved about deep down inside him. He knew, he was certain, that he was supposed to paint something. Perhaps the picture of his life. The strange affair of Miss Graveley's hair; the dead hedgehog; and now this lonely corpse – surely they were a symbol of life and death? Joy and sorrow. Good and evil. Then there was the bluebottle. . . .

Sam lay down his paints, the easel and the baby hedgehogs and he dragged the corpse into a nearby patch of sunlight, for it was screened from the sun by the rhododendron. When the model was suitably illuminated Sam set up his easel and his stool and sat down to paint.

The dead face of the dead man had given him the

inspiration he needed. The dead face of this man held the millions and millions of dead faces of all the centuries. In that dead face lay all dead humanity; all cold history; all the odd attitudes and mistakes. He would paint the faces of the world that had been. All the thousands of faces massed together. All the staring eyes of the people as they stood wondering, laughing, weeping, and dull with misunderstanding and ignorance. The faces of the Jews and the Gentiles, the Romans and the Egyptians and the Greeks. And beyond them he would paint the people who watched across the years and the centuries; the children at scripture; the teachers; the monks and the politicians; the publicans; the people of every day in every country, all standing looking and not knowing.

Sam Marlow, his eyes fixed on the face of the dead man, mixed his colours and then began to paint. He roughed in a hazy background. A background of one tremendous, gargantuan human face, more dead than the face of the corpse which lay in front of him. So intent was he on his task that he did not notice another human face which slowly materialized amongst the evergreen leaves of the rhododendron. There was nothing dead about this face; this was the face of living humanity; brown, humorous, wrinkled, struggling to accommodate a splendid yawn. At the critical, top-dead-centre of this yawn the eyes focused properly on the young artist and the body; the yawn was lost forever.

''Struth!' said the new captain.

Sam Marlow, painting a delicate line, carefully removed his brush from the canvas, then raised a quizzical eyebrow at the corpse.

The captain said: 'And I was kidding meself it was all a nasty dream!'

Sam then saw the face of the new captain floating in the shrubbery like a puzzle picture in a children's comic. He looked from the captain to the corpse, digesting the captain's remark and considering the implications.

'Is this your body, little man?'

The captain began to emerge from the bush, the gun clasped in his hands. 'Don't give me away! Don't split on me! I thought he was a rabbit or pheasant or something!' By now the little hanging nooses were appearing amongst the trees.

Sam Marlow studied the body; he had a considerable imagination of his own, but he could not see the reason for the captain's error.

'Let's get this straight,' he said.

# The Corpse Made No Reply

Sam Marlow the artist and Albert Wiles the new captain sat down on the warm earth to discuss the unfortunate happening, while close by Harry the corpse lay bootless and silent.

According to the young artist, who was a realist, prepared for every eventuality and surprised by none, the affair was a simple one and there was no cause for alarm. Although the retired lighterman was old enough to be Sam Marlow's father, the young artist spoke to him as though he, the captain, was the junior. He spoke with cool, clear reasoning, but the little captain remained unimpressed. This was to be understood, since the artist could see only the captain and the fine landscape, whereas the captain could see the corpse, the gun, and a number of hanging nooses.

'It stands to reason,' Sam explained, 'that they can't touch you for it. It was accidental. An act of God, perhaps. In a way you should be grateful that you were able to do your share in accomplishing the destiny of a fellow-being.'

The captain stared morosely at the hanging nooses and said nothing. Sam continued:

'Suppose for instance,' he said, 'it was written in the Book of Heaven that this man was to die in this particular place and at this particular time. Suppose for a moment that in some manner the actual accomplishing of his demise had been bungled; that something had gone wrong. Perhaps it was to be a thunderbolt and there was no thunder available, say. Well, you come along and you shoot him and Heaven's will is done and destiny fulfilled. Surely your conscience is quite clear? Why should *you* be unhappy?'

The captain licked his lips and, after a moment, he spoke. He said:

'Now look, Sammy. You got the wrong end of the blooming stick. It's not me conscience that's worrying me. I haven't got a conscience. If you'd been the places I've been and seen the things I've seen *you* wouldn't have a conscience, neither. And it's not Heaven that worries me, for I don't suppose I'll ever have to face it. And it's not his mother or his father neither, which I don't suppose he ever knew. And it's not any of the fine things you've been talking about. It's not nothing like that. It's me. It's me what's worrying me. Me and my neck. I know the police and their suspicious ways. I had a brother in the police and he told me that everybody they has anything to do with is guilty till they're proved innocent – and I don't want nothing to do with 'em. Bury him, I say, and have done with him. He's no good to no one now, not the way he is. Lay him to rest. Put him under the sod. Forget him. You never saw him and I never done it.'

Sam shook his head, sorrowfully. 'And what about all those other people who saw him? How about the woman and the little boy? How about Miss Graveley? The tramp? The man chasing butterflies – that'll be Dr Greenbow. How about the man and the blonde – that'll be Mark Douglas and Mrs D'Arcy. How about them?'

The captain waved his hand as if they didn't mean a thing. 'Nobody was interested,' he said. 'Nobody cared – except you.'

'That's what *you* think,' Sam reasoned. 'But suppose somebody starts to care after you've buried him? It would look bad for you then, I must say. Suppose this woman who called him Harry decides she loves him, after all?'

'Not a chance,' said the captain, remembering the look on her face.

'What was she like?' Sam asked.

'Pretty as a picture,' said the captain.

'With a little boy?'

'Yes.'

'Mrs Rogers,' said Sam.

'So let's bury him,' Captain Wiles suggested.

'I don't like it,' Sam said. 'The authorities like to know when people die. This was an accident and you've got nothing to fear.'

The captain sighed. 'Look,' he said. 'You forget it. You cut along. I killed him and I'll take care of his remains.'

Sam regarded the little man distrustfully. 'And you'll go dragging him round the heath for the rest of the day. If you're not careful you *will* get a murder charge lined up – damned if I don't begin to suspect something myself.'

The captain wilted. 'There you are then, see? If *you* think the worst what are *they* going to think? I don't know him, I tell you. Nobody knows him.'

'What about the envelope?' Sam reminded him. 'You've got his name and address. By rights you should send him back.'

'I'll bury the envelope with him.'

Sam thought. He knew now that he would never paint the picture he had started to paint. He knew that his afternoon was ruined. He thought he might as well devote the remainder of the day to clearing up this small mystery.

'I'll tell you what,' he said.

Captain Wiles looked at him suspiciously.

'I'll tell you what we'll do,' Sam said. 'We'll try to find out how Mrs Rogers knows this man and if she intends to notify the police of his death.'

'What good will that do?' asked the captain.

'A lot of good,' said Sam. 'If she's just a distant friend of his and she doesn't intend to notify the authorities of what has happened then I, personally, will help you to bury the body.'

The captain pondered. He regarded the strong young

frame of the artist and he thought of the work involved in burying a body on a hot day.

'All right,' he conceded. Then he had a sudden thought. 'What's the time?'

Sam looked at the sun. 'Nearly tea-time.'

'I got a date,' said Captain Wiles. 'I got a date with Miss Graveley.'

'Good God!' said Sam, remembering Miss Graveley's excitement and wondering why.

The captain looked at him inquiringly.

'I think you're setting a precedent,' Sam explained.

'I'm not setting nothing,' said the captain. 'I'm going round for a spot of char on her own invitation.'

'You'll be the first man ever to cross her threshold,' Sam said.

'As to that,' the captain said, after giving the statement due consideration, 'I don't know. She's a nice, well-preserved woman, but you have to open preserves some day.' He laughed and slapped the artist's shoulder. 'You trot along down and see what Mrs Rogers has to say, Sammy.'

'How about hiding the body first?' Sam suggested.

'Crikey!' said the captain. 'I should say!'

They got to their feet and looked around. There were many hiding places and it was difficult to choose one. The heath was made of hiding places. A thousand bodies could be hidden in this heath.

'Over there,' said Sam.

'Or over there,' said the captain.

'Or just here,' said Sam.

'Or down there,' said the captain.

'What's wrong with the rhododendron where you were hiding?' said Sam.

'That's the first place *I* thought of,' the captain said.

'It'll be safe enough there till dusk,' said Sam.

They dragged the corpse back towards the rhododendron,

51

taking one bare foot each. As they passed beneath a wide-spreading oak tree somebody sneezed and they knew it wasn't them. They looked up. At first they could see no one, but soon they discerned a man sitting amongst the leaves. He was trying to blow his nose without making a noise but when he saw he had been discovered he gave his nose a good, noisy clear-out.

'Here,' the captain called up to him. 'What're you doing up there?'

The man looked down at the captain and the artist and the body. 'What are you doing down there?' he asked.

Sam and the captain looked at each other across the corpse.

'What shall I say?' whispered the captain.

Sam shrugged. 'You should have minded your own business, then he would have minded his.'

The captain shouted up: 'It's a nice afternoon.'

There was no reply. It was obvious that the man in the tree had no interest in the two men with the body. He was staring at a patch of bracken some distance away which only he, in his elevated position, could see.

Just then the thin man with the butterfly net came crashing along between the shrubbery. Now his face was set with second wind and his legs moved automatically. The same large, coloured butterfly still danced merrily ahead. This Doctor Greenbow was on the little funeral party before they knew it, and before the doctor knew it he was lying flat across the dead body again, while the butterfly trod the air beyond.

The doctor got to his feet, slowly and stiffly.

'I beg your pardon,' he said to the corpse. 'I am most frightfully sorry. Have I hurt you?''

The corpse made no reply, but just lay there, waiting for Sam and the captain to put it back under the rhododendron.

'It's quite all right, doctor,' Sam said. 'I'll take care of him. You get along now – you're keeping your butterfly waiting.'

The tall, thin man jumped to his feet, suddenly aware of the rest of the company. His face widened a trifle, in appreciation. 'Thank you,' he said, and was gone.

Sam and the captain bent again to their task, while the man in the tree gazed across the bracken.

# A Nice Cup of Tea

Mr D'Arcy – Mr Walter D'Arcy – sat in the tree and watched his wife sporting with Mr Douglas, and when it had reached a certain stage he climbed down from the tree and went home, filled with a desire and a design for justice, for he was a solicitor's clerk.

Walter D'Arcy was a man who lived beyond his capabilities. He took on more than he could manage, bit off more than he could chew, and leaped before he looked. As a result of this unfortunate trait he had got to forty slightly the worse for wear, with a permanently ruffled appearance.

He had married the blonde quite lately and in a fit of bravado. He had become attached to her in the way a dog becomes attached to its mistress. He resented the intrusion of Mark Douglas as a dog resents the alienation of its mistress's affection. He had stayed home that afternoon to spy on his wife. If his suspicions were well-founded he planned to give Mr Douglas a taste of his own medicine. He had watched the Douglas's home for these past few weeks and from what he had seen he gathered that Mrs Douglas was no more pleased with Mr Douglas than Walter was. In fact, he gathered that the quiet little woman was in much the same frame of mind as he was.

Therefore Walter D'Arcy sat down when he got home and penned a short letter. And being a solicitor's clerk the letter said:

Dear Madam,

At the top of the woodland path on the right, there stands a large oak tree. If you will be in the aforesaid place at dusk tonight you may hear something to your advantage.

Yours faithfully,

A FRIEND.

When he had written this letter and sealed it, knowing Mr Douglas would not be home, he put on his cycle clips and free-wheeled down the woodland path to the Douglas's bungalow, the 'Love Nest', which stood opposite to Mrs Wiggs' cottage.

Walter found Mrs Douglas in the garden. She came to the gate and took the letter from him. She was neither puzzled nor interested, for she had a cloud of gloom in her mind.

'On holiday?' said Mrs Douglas as she took the letter.

Walter pressed her fingers and winked at her. 'I've been for a walk,' he said.

Mrs Douglas blushed, for it was the first time in years that someone had pressed her fingers and winked at her. She was an attractive woman gone careless, like a rose with the old blooms hanging. Her husband had paid her no attention at all for so long that she had forgotten the reason for living. Once, in a fit of wit, he had said that housewives put up with the same thing day after day for the sake of the same thing night after night, and she had agreed with him. But now there was nothing to put up with, for Mark Douglas was continually free-lancing.

'Is there any reply to this?' she said.

'That's up to you, Cassy,' Walter said recklessly.

Mrs Douglas looked at him and began to wonder and as he rode away on his bicycle she opened the letter.

Sam Marlow walked down to 'Chaos' carrying the baby hedgehogs wrapped in a piece of canvas.

Mrs Rogers met him at the front door, for she had seen him from the window. She smiled at him as she stood there in the little porch and the sun was on her face and hair.

She said: 'Good afternoon.'

Sam stepped back to get a better picture. 'You're wonderful,' he said softly. 'You're beautiful, too. You're the most wonderful, beautiful thing I've ever seen.'

Mrs Rogers inclined her head, accepting his praise but not letting it upset her. 'Was there something you wanted, Mr ... er ... Marlow, isn't it?'

'You really are a lovely woman, you know,' Sam informed her. He stepped forward and lifted her dress so that he could see her knees. 'I would like to see you nude,' he said thoughtfully.

She nodded. 'Some other time,' she said. 'I'm just getting Abie's tea.'

'Yes. Yes, of course,' Sam said understandingly, dropping the skirt of her frock. 'Of course. Perhaps I've come at an awkward moment?'

'If you want to undress me, you have,' Mrs Rogers said.

'It wasn't that,' Sam said, trying to remember why he had called.

'Well, come in,' she said. 'Perhaps you would like a cup of tea?'

'I'd love that. Thank you.'

He followed her into the little bungalow and spread himself in a chair by the window. The small boy, Abie, came into the room carrying a dead rabbit. Sam looked at the rabbit and remembered the parcel under his arm. He unwrapped the little hedgehogs and placed them on the floor, where they tried to roll themselves into a ball but were not old enough to know how.

'Hedgehogs!' said Abie delightedly.

'Rabbit,' replied Sam, taking the dead rabbit and stroking it.

'Fleas!' exclaimed the young Mrs Rogers, and she took

up the hedgehogs and carried them out into the garden, stopping to wash her hands at the tap on her way back. Abie followed her out and knelt down watching the baby animals. When Mrs Rogers came back into the room, carrying a steaming cup of tea, Sam said: 'I'm sorry. They're little orphans.'

She smiled at him again and he enjoyed it.

'What's your name?' he said, when he was drinking the tea.

'Jennifer,' she told him. 'Jennifer Rogers.'

He turned this name over in his mind and it satisfied him. 'Who's the man up on the heath?' he said.

'What man?' she said.

'You know – Harry. The dead man.'

She screwed up her nose a little. 'Oh, him. That's my husband.'

'Your husband's dead then?' Sam asked politely.

She nodded. 'Is your tea sweet enough?' she said.

'Yes, thank you,' Sam told her.

Abie came in and took the dead rabbit out of Sam's hand, then went out of the front door.

'Don't be long,' Jennifer Rogers said. 'Your tea's ready.'

'Is Harry Abie's father, then?' Sam asked.

She shook her head emphatically. 'Abie's father is dead,' she said sadly.

'So is Harry.'

'Yes, thank goodness,' she said. She said it as if she were saying grace. 'He was too good to live.'

'He doesn't look as if he were very good,' Sam remarked.

'He was horribly good,' she assured him.

'I like your mouth, too,' Sam said.

'Will you have some more tea?' Jennifer asked him.

'Thanks,' Sam said. Then he added: 'Where's Abie gone?'

'He's gone to see the new captain,' she said. 'He shot that rabbit this afternoon and Abie found it.'

'I'd like to hear some of your life story,' Sam said, 'if you don't mind. You see, we don't know quite what to do with Harry. You may have some suggestions.'

# The Truth About Harry

'You can stuff him for all I care,' Jennifer said. 'Stuff him and put him in a glass case – but I should have frosted glass.'

'You don't like him at all, do you? What did he do besides marry you?'

'Look,' Jennifer said, sitting on the arm of the artist's chair. 'I've wanted to explain about Harry a lot of times, but nobody could understand, least of all Harry. But you – you've got an artistic mind. You can see the finer things.'

Sam agreed with her. 'Tell me everything, Jennifer.'

The woman's eyes hazed. 'It was a long time ago,' she said, 'and I was in love. I was too much in love. But I was young and he was younger.'

'How long ago was this?' Sam asked.

'Let's see,' she said. 'How old is Abie? . . . Four . . . that's right; it would be about four years ago.'

'You *were* in love, weren't you?' Sam remarked.

'We were going to get married,' Jennifer explained. 'It was all arranged. We had agreed to overlook each other's families and everything. And then Robert got killed . . .'

She paused, and it was a tearful pause, full of might-have-beens.

'That was terrible for you,' said Sam.

She sighed. 'I was heartbroken,' she said, 'for six weeks – then I discovered I was going to have a baby.'

'That was embarrassing,' said Sam.

'And that was where Harry came in,' said Jennifer. 'Harry the Handsome Hero. Harry the Saint. Harry the Good.'

'Who was this Harry?' Sam asked.

'Robert's brother,' she said, 'his elder brother.'

'He fell in love with you?'

She made a derisive sound with her mouth. 'If he had fallen in love with me I wouldn't have minded. But he wanted to marry me simply because I was in a jam. And because it was his brother who had put me in a jam.'

'Harry wanted some of the jam,' said Sam.

She nodded darkly. 'I didn't guess. I thought he loved me. I thought he had been silently suffering all the time Robert and I had been courting. I thought he loved me to desperation and though I didn't think much of him I decided to let him marry me for the sake of giving Abie a name.' She fell silent and Sam sipped his second cup of tea. Then she looked down at him and there was a minor tragedy in her eyes. 'It was on my wedding night I learned the truth.'

'That's when most people learn the truth,' Sam remarked.

'But this was a terrible truth,' Jennifer said. 'This was the truth about Harry.'

'What happened?'

'How old are you, Mr Marlow?'

'About twenty-nine.'

'This is what happened,' she said, softly and secretly. 'I had undressed . . .'

'Go on,' Sam encouraged.

'I had undressed,' she continued, 'and donned my nightie. I went up to bed first, you understand.'

'I understand perfectly,' Sam said.

'Although I had no true feeling for Harry I had worked myself into a certain enthusiasm because I thought he loved me.'

'It must have been hard work,' Sam said.

Jennifer was back to her wedding night and going strong. She said: 'I sat by the window and there was a moon. I didn't get into bed because I wanted him to see my new nightie.'

'Naturally,' Sam said.

Jennifer returned to Sam for a moment. 'I don't know why I'm telling you all this – you a perfect stranger, too. I'm not boring you, am I?'

'Not at all,' Sam said politely.

'Have some more tea?'

'Soon,' said Sam. 'Soon.'

'Where was I?' Jennifer asked.

'You were sitting by the window and there was a moon. You hadn't got into bed because you wanted him to see your new nightie. You had worked yourself into a certain enthusiasm.'

Jennifer laughed lightly. 'Did I say all that?'

'When does Harry come in?' Sam asked her impatiently.

Her face straightened and the mirth left her. 'At last,' she said, 'Harry came in.'

'What had he been doing all this time?' Sam said, petulantly.

'Finding a picture of Robert,' Jennifer said.

'Robert!'

'Robert,' Jennifer repeated. 'A photograph of my dead lover. A photograph of the father of my child. A photograph of his brother.'

'Why did he want that?' Sam asked.

'That's what I wanted to know. It wasn't even a good photograph. He said ... I hardly like to tell you what he said.'

'I'd like to hear it,' Sam encouraged her.

'He said,' she said, '"I'm going to hang dear Robert over our bed, dear. You are bearing his child, remember. So when I make love to you, Jenny, I want you to imagine that it's really Robert making love to you."'

Sam was shocked. 'He said that?'

She nodded soberly. 'I was going to imagine it was Robert, anyway,' she said, 'but I didn't want him to imagine that I was imagining it was Robert.'

'I should think not!'

'And,' said Jennifer, 'he didn't as much as mention my new nightie.'

'What did you do?' Sam asked.

'I left him,' she said. 'I went round to mother's straight away. So I never *did* have to imagine it was Robert and now I never shall.'

'What a poignant story,' Sam said.

Jennifer smiled sadly at him. 'I knew you would understand – nobody else does. Even mother thought I should live with him. But I wouldn't. He pestered me to go back, but I always refused. At last he even offered to take down the photograph over the bed, but it was too late.'

'I don't blame you,' Sam said.

'Abie was born,' Jennifer said, 'and as soon as I could I moved away to where I thought Harry would never find me. I changed my name –'

'But he did find you?'

'Yes. Today.'

'Yesterday?'

'No. Today. This morning. There was a knock on the door and there he was. Harry.'

'What did he want?'

'At last,' Jennifer said, 'he wanted me. Not on his brother's account, either, but on his own account. He had suddenly felt a basic urge, he said. He wanted me because I was his wife.'

'How did you feel about it?' Sam asked.

'I felt sick,' said the young woman. 'Did you see his moustache and his wavy hair?'

Sam agreed with her. 'But when *I* saw him,' he said, 'he was dead.'

Jennifer shrugged. 'He looked exactly the same when he was alive, except that he was vertical.'

'What did you say to him?' Sam asked.

'Nothing,' Jennifer said. 'I hit him on the head with a milk bottle and knocked him silly.'

'How do you mean "silly"?'

'Silly-dilly,' she said. 'Bats. He went staggering up towards the heath saying he was going to find his wife.'

'So he turned human at the last?' Sam asked.

'He did,' she said. 'But he was too late as far as I was concerned.'

'I'll have another cup of tea,' Sam said.

While she was preparing it for him he sat back and thought.

# Mirage

'The Ship' was a thing of stucco, breeze blocks and cheap Canadian timber. It lay at anchor in its little garden amongst the trees. It lay in the heat of the summer afternoon, looking not merely becalmed but derelict. The portholes were dusty, being draped with a grey material that might have been curtain or cobweb. The paintwork was worn and cracked by the weather, unwashed and covered by the colourless, dried drippings from leaves on hundreds of past wet days. It was a bungalow that had suffered abominably from bachelors.

The three rooms that comprised the inside of this residence were stuffed with untidiness. Every possible hiding place for odds and ends had been thought of and used. Every item of furniture that nobody could ever find a use for had been gathered together in those three rooms. Outside, in the small shed, four tea-chests of personal belongings, mostly junk, stood still packed, while the more treasured of these relics took pride of place in all the corners of the rooms, filling the bungalow with riverside memories spread over some thirty years. Relics that ranged from a life-belt that had saved Albert Wiles's life, to the suspender belt of a Deptford barmaid who had almost wrecked it. So crammed with stuff was this bungalow that only by habitual movement from room to room could the captain keep a space free for movement.

When at five o'clock on this pleasant summer afternoon Captain Wiles stepped out of this mess and muddle, looking spry and spruce, it was the miracle of the new-laid egg leaving the bowels of a scruffy old hen. For some strange reason he had taken greater pains with his personal appearance than ever before, greater even than on that famous occasion when he had set out to meet Gertie at Gravesend with the intention of cutting out his old rival, Tiger Wray. It was strange because this Miss Graveley bore no comparison to Gertie of Gravesend, who had been young, supple and red-haired. But then the captain was no longer young and supple and by this time Gertie, who had eventually married Tiger and borne him seven cubs, was even less young and supple.

These thoughts chased each other through the captain's mind as he came to the hollyhocks of 'The Haven'. These and other thoughts. He compared this trim little bungalow with his own. The white muslin curtains with the bright embroidery, the shining blue paintwork of the window frames and door, the organized splendour of the garden. And with it all he remembered her nice, grey eyes and her dark hair. And in his memory the old-fashioned 'bun' vanished and instead he saw bright ribbon amongst gay but dignified curls; her eyes shone brightly and her mouth was a colour that matched the ribbon, while her cheeks were the candy-pink of the hollyhocks.

These thoughts took no ordered or conscious significance in his mind, for all his life he had thought of a woman as a woman, a house as a house, and a garden as a home for cabbages. Nothing more or less. He was a man of the world with a broad mind, human impulses and a convenient conscience; he had always found marriage entirely unnecessary. But in some vague and disquieting way the sounds of the woodlands now held a hint of wedding bells, and the captain knew that it was because his memory was lying. He knew it was the ribbon and the bright eyes and the pink cheeks.

He knocked at the door of 'The Haven' and then stood back with a smile on his soap-shone face and his shoulders squared, viewing his reflection approvingly in the shiny paintwork. When Miss Graveley answered his knock she did so from behind him, for she had been cutting the roses which she held in her arms.

'Here you are, then,' she said.

The captain swung around and his pose was wasted. He felt as if he had been caught pulling faces at himself in the mirror. Then he forgot his embarrassment and lost himself in the picture of the woman as she stood framed by the porch against the garden. His memory had been perfectly accurate. There were the curls and the ribbon and the pink cheeks and the bright eyes. And there, also, far beyond the buzzing of bees and the bored chirp of a bird, were those bells again.

'Yes, ma'am,' he said, removing his cap.

# Do You Want to Sell a Rabbit?

Abie Rogers was trying to make somebody answer his knocking at the door of 'The Ship'. For a small boy he was able to kick up a terrific din with the aid of a rusty saucepan-lid he had found on the front path.

He banged and nobody came. He banged again, and again nobody came. He kept this up for five minutes and then put the dead rabbit down by the front door and walked back up the garden path. When he got to the gate he looked back and saw a cat sniffing at the small corpse. Abie threw the saucepan-lid with great accuracy and it landed with a clatter right beside the cat. The cat, a large tabby animal belonging to the captain, recognized this saucepan-lid as one which had been tied to its tail for the greater part of yesterday and, resigned yet curiously forgiving, it scuttled away, expecting the lid to follow.

Abie came back and picked up the rabbit. He stood idly stroking its fur and wondering what could have happened to the new captain. As he stood there the quiet sounds of the woods were augmented by a laugh. It was a man's laugh and it seemed to come from beyond the hollyhocks of 'The Haven'. He made no immediate move, for common sense told him that no man could possibly be in 'The Haven'. 'The Haven' was where Miss Graveley lived and Miss Gravely spoke only to women and girls and boys under twelve.

Soon again the laugh was airborne and Abie's hunter's sense overcame his common sense and told him that the new captain was indeed visiting his neighbour. With the rabbit hanging by its feet in one hand he walked down the woodland path to Miss Graveley's bungalow. He walked around the bungalow and when he got to the sitting-room window he saw Miss Graveley and her guest sitting on either side of a most attractive tea, which included several kinds of cake. Abie stepped into view and held aloft the dead rabbit. His eyes were fixed unswervingly on the cakes.

When Miss Graveley caught sight of Abie and the rabbit she got up and opened the window fully. 'Well, little man,' she said, 'and do you want to sell a rabbit?'

'It belongs to the new captain,' Abie said, dipping his head a trifle to keep the cakes in view.

The captain reached the window in half a stride. 'What's that?'

Abie handed him the rabbit without losing sight of the cakes. 'You killed it,' he said absently, 'with your gun.'

The captain held the rabbit away from him and squinted at it, as though it were a rare oil painting.

Miss Graveley watched him with some slight amusement in her eyes. 'You must have shot it this afternoon. It will make a nice supper for you.'

The new captain did not reply, for he was almost beyond words. And this was strange, because he had just been recounting to his hostess an abundance of tall stories relating to near squeezes and narrow scrapes in distant and dangerous lands. But Captain Wiles, who had never done any of these things, but had long cherished an ambition to shoot a rabbit, was sent completely out of his head by this little furry victim. He parted the fur and examined the bullet wound. He felt for the rabbit's pulse. He looked into its dead eyes. His face turned white and crimson in ten-second cycles. He breathed deeply and ecstatically. He tried to say something to Abie and failed. He tried to say something to Miss Graveley and failed. He was completely incoherent for several minutes, during which time Abie stood outside the window watching the cakes and Miss Graveley stood inside the window watching the captain and smiling indulgently. Mingled with this indulgence was a certain fondness. Such excited behaviour in a man of his years was an endearing quality.

At last Captain Wiles held the rabbit aloft and found his voice. 'I've killed a rabbit! I've killed a blooming rabbit!' Then he reached through the window and ruffled the little boy's hair. 'Where'd you find it, sonny?'

'On the cake,' said Abie promptly.

'Eh?'

'On the heath,' said Abie.

Miss Graveley got Abie a large slice of cake and the small boy retreated gratefully. The captain went slowly back to his chair, stroking the fur of his small victim. 'I must tell Sam about this,' he murmured. At that moment his pleasure in the rabbit reached out and embraced his pleasure in all things; in meeting Sam Marlow; in making young Mrs Rogers so happy with the small accident to Harry; in providing shoes for the tramp. Especially in meeting Miss Graveley and hearing the bells. Impulsively he laid his hand on hers and said : 'It's a nice afternoon, ma'am.'

She responded by putting her other hand on his arm. 'And I think you're awfully nice, Captain Wiles, even when you're lying to me.'

The Captain opened his mouth to expostulate or something, but Miss Graveley placed a finger across his lips and he said nothing. They exchanged a look. It was the look of an adult man to an adult woman in an adult world.

# Nice People

The sun lay low across the heath when Captain Wiles and Sam arrived with their spades. The bracken and the shrubbery cast long shadows and small rabbits started in the short grass and quickly hopped back to cover.

Peering into the heart of the rhododendron, the captain said: 'He seems comfortable, Sam. Very comfortable and snug.'

Sam said: 'We'd better find a place to bury him and get it dug. The sooner he's underground the better.'

'If what you've been telling me is right,' the captain remarked, 'I agree with you, Sammy.'

They walked the heath looking for a lonely and secluded spot where the earth was soft for digging. Sam led the way into bracken that stood higher than the rest, thick and above their heads. The little captain stumbled after him, picking his feet through bramble and ducking his head under the coarse vegetation.

'This looks a good place,' said Sam, stooping.

They surveyed the prospective graveyard. It was completely enclosed by the bracken and overlooked only by the sky. It was almost as gloomy here as it had been under the rhododendron. The ground was a soft bed of black leaf-mould.

'Seems too nice a place to bury a bloke like that,' Captain Wiles whispered. 'Wouldn't mind being buried here meself.'

'One at a time, please,' Sam whispered, taking off his jacket.

The captain watched him while he began clearing the

leaf-mould away with his spade. Suddenly conscious of his audience Sam looked up at him. 'Well, come on – off with your coat.'

'What, me?'

'Yes, of course – it's your body.'

They dug. They dug and they sweated. They dug violently and silently and the damp, black mould came up in heavy clods. Gradually, very gradually, they worked their way into an oblong hole, casting up a tremendous pile of earth on either side.

Soon the captain was having to manoeuvre his spadeful of earth up and over his shoulder. He worked gamely on till it was no longer possible. Then with a last despairing heave he flung the spade out of the hole and collapsed against the earth wall.

'What's the trouble?' Sam asked, through a curtain of perspiration.

'Dead beat,' said the captain, panting.

'Good,' Sam said. 'I was dead beat ten minutes ago, but I wanted to keep on till your last gasp.'

The captain tried to climb out but only succeeded in fetching a lot of earth back into the hole.

'Don't do that,' Sam said, 'Or you'll get your wish and be buried here yourself. Here, I'll give you a hand up.'

Sam took Captain Wiles by the seat of his pants and hoisted him out, then followed up himself. They stood looking down into the hole and it was big and deep and black, smelling strongly of earth.

'Fair gives me the creeps,' said the captain.

'Let's go and call for Harry then,' Sam said, leading the way back through the bracken.

They carried the body of Harry between them and it was as stiff as a plank. Sam took the head and shoulders and the captain the bare feet. They got it into the bracken as soon as they could for fear of meeting somebody who might wonder what they were doing.

The journey from the rhododendron to the grave, which was no more than fifty yards as the crow flies, seemed to take a small eternity, for it was no easy matter to push the bracken aside with the head, keep the feet clear of brambles, and at the same time hold the body securely. And when at last they lowered the corpse into the grave it was, in that grim spot, almost dark.

'After this,' Sam remarked, as they straightened their backs, 'if you must kill, stick to rabbits. The corpse is smaller.'

Captain Wiles, who had begun to push the earth over Harry's face, suddenly swung around and cried: 'Rabbits! I didn't tell you, did I, Sammy? I shot a flipping rabbit this afternoon. Killed it stone dead.'

'Don't shout,' Sam cautioned. 'I know you did. I was with Jennifer when Abie took it round to you.'

'Jennifer, eh?' said the captain, helping to cover up the body. 'You didn't waste much time, did you? Still, I don't blame you. A very nice widow she'll make, I don't doubt. Very nice indeed.'

'Let's talk about that when we've finished burying Harry, shall we?' Sam said, as Harry's face vanished beneath the soil.

'No need to get huffy,' said the captain. 'I don't want to talk about your affairs – I've got affairs of my own.'

Sam slung a glance at him. 'You mean my protégée?'

'Come again,' said the captain.

'Miss Graveley,' said Sam. 'The lady I renovated down at Mrs Wiggs' this afternoon. A most remarkable reversion to femininity, that.'

The captain stopped digging and leaned on his spade. 'I don't quite get you, Sammy boy.'

Sam also leaned on his spade. They faced each other across the gloom of the grave. 'She came down to the Emporium in high excitement,' he said. 'Wanted ribbon for her hair and a new cup and all kinds of things. I gave her a little make - up and a new hair - style – don't say you didn't notice.?'

The captain scratched his chin. 'Funny,' he said, reflectively. 'I must have had what they call a preview, Sammy. When I saw her on the heath this afternoon – that was just after I'd shot Harry – I wasn't struck by her femin – feminit – what you said; but when I got to thinking about her later on I saw her just the way she was when I went to tea.'

'I think that's significant,' Sam said.

'She's a very nice lady, Sam. *Very* nice.'

'We're all nice,' Sam said, resuming his digging. 'I don't see how anyone could fail to like us.'

'That's the way I feel today, Sammy.' Captain Wiles fell to with fresh energy. 'I don't know if I've grown rose-coloured glasses or if –'

'Or if it's love,' said Sam, whacking the earth down on Harry with the back of the spade.

'What did Jennifer think of my shooting?' the captain asked, smoothing the ground level and raking dead bracken over it.

'You mean Mrs Rogers?' Sam corrected him.

'I don't know about Mrs Rogers,' said the captain. 'I reckon I can count myself a friend of the family. I brought her a happy release with one bullet.'

'One bullet?' said Sam. 'How about the hedgehog?'

'One bullet for the hedgehog, one for the paper bag, and one for Harry,' said the captain with dignity.

'How about the rabbit?' Sam inquired.

'And one for the rab –'

Captain Wiles stopped short and Sam Marlow looked at him questioningly. The little man was standing with a stupid expression on his face, counting his fingers. Slowly he turned and his eyes were wide and incredulous.

'What's the matter?' Sam asked.

The captain took up his spade and began removing the leaf-mould from Harry's grave.

73

'Hey! What's wrong? What's bitten you?' Sam demanded.

'Three bullets I fired,' muttered the captain. 'Three. One for the hedgehog, one for the bag, one for the –'

'The little man who's lying in the grave,' chanted Sam.

'No, Sammy. That's just it. One for the rabbit. I shot the rabbit. If I shot the rabbit I didn't shoot Harry. What have you made me do, Sammy boy? Sam Marlow, you've made a murderer out of me.' He was digging feverishly into the earth in search of Harry.

Sam sat down amongst the bracken and watched him. He felt there was little he could say.

'Don't sit there!' the captain implored over his shoulder. 'You helped to bury him.'

At last Sam said, reasonably: 'Even if you didn't kill him, why go digging him up now he's nicely planted? I promised Jennifer we'd bury him and buried he must be. Besides, whether you killed him or not, you've incriminated yourself. You'll have more of a job explaining away a body you buried and didn't kill than a body you killed accidentally and buried. You're not supposed to bury bodies when you find them. It makes people so suspicious. You should take them to the police or advertise or something.'

'Oh, Sam, you don't understand. You don't comprehend one little bit. You wouldn't have me go all through my life not knowing if I've killed him or not?'

'You're being very inconsistent,' Sam said. 'First you tell me you have no conscience, then you talk of something that sounds remarkably like a conscience.'

'Come and help me, Sammy,' the captain pleaded. 'I don't care if I killed him or not, as far as that goes, but I'll get the willies every time I see a policeman and it's no good saying I won't. You wouldn't want me to go the rest of my life with the willies when it isn't strictly necessary, would you?'

Sam shrugged. The captain cast him one miserable glance before ducking below the level of the ground.

Sam lit half of a cigarette and waited. Soon the captain's head bobbed up again. 'I've got one arm,' he said. 'Help me pull him out.'

Sam sighed and got up.

Presently Harry lay on the brink of his recent grave. He was little the worse for his brief interment it seemed, suffering only a quantity of black soil in his hair.

'Strike a match,' said the captain.

Sam struck a match.

'Hold it over here, near the blood.'

Sam held the match near the forehead of the corpse.

'This isn't a bullet wound,' exclaimed Captain Wiles. 'It's what they call a blow with a blunt instrument.'

Sam flicked the match away into the bracken and watched it go out. He puffed at his cigarette and inhaled, deeply, then blew the smoke at a persistent mosquito.

The captain watched him, for right at that moment he was feeling singularly lacking in self-confidence.

'Sam?' he said tentatively.

Sam raised an eyebrow.

'What do you think, Sam?' asked Captain Wiles.

'I think, little man,' said Sam, 'that we are tangled in murder.'

'If it's murder,' said Captain Wiles, 'who done it?'

'Who did it,' Sam corrected.

'That's what I say. Who done it? Apart from Jennifer, who would want to kill him?'

'Apart from Jennifer . . .' Sam murmured.

The captain studied him. 'You don't think –'

'Don't be ridiculous,' Sam told him. 'You said yourself she was surprised to find the body.'

'You said she hit him on the head,' the captain accused. 'I've heard of a case where a bloke bumped his head on a brick wall and fell dead two days later.'

'Probably knocked down by a bus,' Sam said. 'No, it wasn't Jennifer. Look here, what does it matter who did it – he'll be best buried and out of the way.'

'I don't think!' said the captain. 'I'm not burying someone else's bad habits.'

'Suppose it was Miss Graveley?' Sam suggested.

The captain was silent for a moment, then he laughed and the sound of it went away through the bracken and came back as an echo.

'It's not as funny as all that,' Sam said, 'She didn't seem particularly startled when she saw you dragging that body up the path.'

The captain shook his head at Sam. 'You artists haven't got no idea of etiquette. Miss Graveley is a lady of gentle manners and upbringing. A lady to hide her feelings. If I hadn't been holding Harry by his ankles I don't suppose she would have mentioned him, even. When she said: "Been shooting?" it wasn't no more than a pleasantry, so to speak, like saying "Nice day, I'm sure", or something like that –'

'Going to help me bury him again?' Sam said. 'It might have been Miss Graveley, or the tramp, or Mark Douglas, or Mrs D'Arcy, or –'

'Jennifer,' said the captain.

'I've told you –' Sam broke off and shrugged. 'It's not worth arguing about. Let's get rid of him.'

The captain pushed Harry with his foot and the corpse rolled over the brink of the grave, dropping in the soft bottom with a dull thud. 'There you are, then. I've done my share,' he said.

Sam picked up a spade.

# The Lovers' Nest

The sun went down and the moon came up like some ponderous juggling act. Sparrowswick Heath took on wonderful shades of copper and blue and silver under the four high corners of the sky.

Beneath the oak tree near the top of the woodland path Walter D'Arcy met Mrs Douglas. The little woman came to him with a question in her eyes and he took her walking into the bracken to answer it.

Soon Captain Albert Wiles, newly shaved and shone, came walking along with Miss Graveley. Now the captain was subdued, for he knew she was not fooled and that if he had anything to say it would have to be sincere.

When they had vanished, Sam Marlow, Jennifer and Abie came out of the wood and strolled along the heath path like a little after-supper family. Jennifer wore a white linen dress with a scarlet belt, while Sam wore a clean cricket shirt and a pair of trousers with the suggestion of a crease in them. Abie stalked on ahead, using his stalkingest steps and peering bravely amongst the shadows.

Soon Abie came to where he had discovered the man with the blood on his face. He stopped.

'What's the matter?' Sam asked, coming level with him.

'It's where he found Harry,' Jennifer said. 'Come along; don't let's be morbid.'

'Get up, you brute!' said Abie.

His mother tugged at his shoulder. 'Abie!'

'Right!' said Abie reminiscently. 'Now you've asked for it!'

They then walked on in silence, for the memory of Harry had thrown a little gloom over them.

'I wonder why Abie said that, just at that particular spot,' remarked Sam.

Jennifer did not wonder anything at all, for she was admiring the tangerine moon and what it did to the earth and the sky.

'Abie,' said Sam presently.

'Yes, Marlow?' said Abie.

'Call him Sam,' his mother commanded, coming out of her reverie.

'Yes, Sam?' said Abie obediently.

'Who said: "Get up, you brute"?'

'The lady in the lovers' nest,' said Abie promptly.

'What is a lovers' nest?' asked Sam, considerably puzzled.

Jennifer broke in at that stage and she sounded embarrassed. 'I told him that,' she confessed. 'He came home the other day and said he'd seen ... er ... certain of our neighbours sitting together in the bracken.'

'Lying, Mummy,' said Abie.

'I see,' said Sam. 'And who was this lady in the lovers' nest, Abie? The one who said "Get up, you brute"?'

'I don't know,' Abie said.

'Where was this nest?' Sam asked.

Abie stopped and pointed back the way they had come.

Sam turned and began retracting his steps. 'Come and show me,' he said. They walked until they came to where Harry had lain. 'Was it here?' Sam said.

Abie nodded emphatically. Sam looked at Jennifer, but she seemed not a bit interested.

She said: 'He means the other day.'

'I'm not so sure,' Sam said. 'When did you see this lovers' nest?' he asked Abie.

'The other day,' said Abie.

'*This* one?' Sam said.

'Tomorrow,' Abie said, after consideration.

Jennifer laughed. 'You'll never make sense out of Abie; he's got his own timing and it's nothing like Greenwich. Anyway, why not let sleeping toads lie?'

'Now that we know the captain didn't do it,' Sam said, 'wouldn't you like to know who did?'

'Why look a gift horse or something in the mouth?' Jennifer said, glancing around to recapture the moon.

'Look, Abie,' said Sam, turning to the little boy. 'When the lady said what she said, where exactly was she?'

'In the lovers' nest.'

'And where is the lovers' nest?'

'Here,' said Abie, pointing down to the trampled grass and bracken.

'And when was it?'

Abie hesitated over this. 'Soon,' he said at last.

'What did the man say?' Sam asked, undismayed.

'Right, now you've asked for it!' said Abie.

'And where was the man –'

'*Sam!*' said Jennifer impatiently. 'For heaven's sake!'

Sam waved her aside and repeated his question.

'In the lovers' nest,' said Abie, speaking as if taking part in some parlour game.

'And where is the lovers' nest?'

'Just here,' said Abie.

'And what were you doing?' Sam said.

'Lying down,' said Abie.

'Why?' asked Sam.

'The new captain was shooting at me,' Abie said, proudly.

'And where did you find the rabbit?'

Abie looked around, then pointed along the path. 'Just down there.'

'And which did you find first, the man or the rabbit?'

'The man,' said Abie, 'but I couldn't pick him up.'

Jennifer started walking away. 'Come on. I don't like this spot.'

'Just a minute,' Sam said. He walked a little way into the bracken and Jennifer watched him. He could see it had been beaten down, but it was too dark to see very much else. He struck a match and before shining it in front of him he lit a half of a cigarette. When the match had illuminated the beaten-down bracken he said: 'Come here, Jennifer.'

The young woman came and stood by his side, look-down at the ground. 'Seems as though he put up a fight. I wonder why,' she commented.

Sam held the dwindling light between their faces. Through the flame he said: 'It looks as though *someone* put up a fight.'

Jennifer thought about that for a little while and the match went out. 'You mean – you think he was with a . . . companion? A woman?'

'Could be,' Sam said.

'I think perhaps you're right,' Jennifer said, leading the way back to where Abie was guarding the path. 'Harry was in a most peculiar mood when I saw him last.'

'Would you say frustrated?'

'I think you might call it that,' Jennifer said.


When Sam Marlow, Jennifer and Abie walked away, Mark Douglas and Mrs D'Arcy came out from behind a tree. They stood viewing the pocket of broken bracken for a moment and the blonde said: 'What on *earth* was all that about?'

Mark Douglas said: 'They seemed to be making a mystery out of this patch of bracken.'

The blonde giggled. 'But how incredibly juvenile!'

# My Crime on Your Conscience

Captain Albert Wiles, ex-lighterman of the Thames barges, sat with Miss Graveley and looked up at the moon with a great deal of satisfaction. They sat together on a fallen tree in one of the little pools of silky grass. The captain puffed at his pipe and marvelled at the amazing convenience of life.

'Funny, y'know,' he said.

Miss Graveley looked at him, politely. He puffed again, manufacturing a small cloud of silver-blue smoke through which he regarded her, kindly and gratefully.

'Funny the way we've got all friendly in one afternoon. I knew you wasn't as prim and starchy as they made out, mind, not by a long chalk.'

'Really?' said Miss Graveley.

'I'm a man as can recognize the human qualities in a woman,' said the captain, switching his gaze to the moon and beyond the moon to Deptford and the Thames reaches. 'When I first saw you and your trim little craft down there behind the hollyhocks I said to myself –'

'Captain Wiles.' Miss Graveley interrupted his flow of talk to save herself further acute embarrassment.

'Ma'am?' The captain was back to earth again and feeling a little apprehensive. He had to remember that what was considered a good line in Limehouse might easily be a *faux pas* on Sparrowswick Heath.

'Before you make your kind thoughts known to me,' said Miss Graveley, now studying her feet, 'I would like to offer you some explanation of my sudden invitation to tea – and my walking with you here this evening –'

'No, ma'am!' exclaimed the captain, holding up his hand in protest. 'You don't have to explain nothing, ma'am. You come to my aid at a time of crisis, ma'am, for which I'm truly grateful. If I was being at all familiar, or speaking out of turn, as they say, then I'm sorry. The truth is, ma'am, I'm a man of few words. A clumsy oaf, you might say, when it comes to expressing appreciation –'

'Not at all, Captain. On the contrary, I find your company delightful. It's just that I owe you some reason –'

'I won't hear of it!' The captain said. 'If you think I think I shall get a wrong opinion of you for asking me to tea and to walk, then I assure you I won't, ma'am. You saw the predicament I was in this afternoon – with that body on my hands and so on – and you shut your eyes to it in a proper sporty fashion, if I may say so –'

'It was about the ... er ... body that I wished to speak ...'

'Say no more!' said the captain. 'I was coming to that myself. I'm glad to tell you that my alarm this afternoon was completely unfounded. The fact is, I lost my head, not being used to shooting people in cold blood, y'understand –'

'Captain Wiles!' said Miss Graveley, with sudden determination and firmness.

'Yes, ma'am?' said the captain.

'I am trying to tell you that I asked you to tea because I felt –'

'Sympathy!' exclaimed the captain. 'Ah, I know a sympathetic woman when I meet one. Sympathy, and sociability and –'

'– gratitude!' exclaimed Miss Graveley, wedging the word so neatly that the captain had to stop and examine it.

'Gratitude?' he said, turning it over. 'I'm the one who should be grateful –'

'No.' Miss Graveley now took control of the conversa-

82

tion. 'I was grateful – I *am* grateful. I'm grateful to you for burying my body.'

The captain now stared at the lady in the moonlight, forgetting to smoke his pipe. At last he said: 'Your body?'

'The man you thought you'd killed,' Miss Graveley explained, 'was the man I hit on the head with my ice-calf brogue.'

The captain could only say: 'You hit Harry on the head with your ice-calf brogue?'

'He annoyed me,' said Miss Graveley, a flush coming to her face at the memory. 'I was walking towards home when he came rushing up to me with a wild look in his eyes and demanded his rights.'

'His rights?' said the captain.

'He tried to make me believe we were married,' she said. 'And believe it or not, Captain Wiles, I had never seen him before in my life – and if I had, I would never have married him!'

'What did he do?' said the captain.

'He pulled me into the bracken –'

'Yes?'

'I came out again –'

'Go on.'

'He pulled me back –'

'He did?'

'He swore at me – horrible, masculine sounds. I didn't understand them, of course –'

'Course not!' said the captain, seething with indignation at the thought of it.

'We fought,' said Miss Graveley, looking away into the night, her face grim, her hands tightly clenched.

'Then what?'

'I won,' said Miss Graveley, not without some pride. 'My shoe had come off in the struggle. I hit him. I hit him as hard as I could – on the temple, where David hit Goliath.'

'And you killed him!' Looking at the middle-aged spinster, the captain found the fact difficult to assimilate.

The lady shrugged. 'I must have done. I was annoyed, Captain. Very annoyed.'

'Naturally,' said the captain.

'I don't think I've ever been so annoyed. Consequently, I didn't realize my own capabilities.'

'Whew!' murmured the captain, looking at her with a new admiration. 'It seems to me that Mrs Rogers knocked him silly and you finished him off.'

Miss Graveley turned a puzzled stare on the little captain, who was now relighting his pipe. 'Why would Mrs Rogers knock him silly?'

'She was really his wife,' the captain said.

'Poor woman!' Miss Graveley said. 'I thought she had better taste.'

'I think she can be exonerated,' said the captain. 'You see ...'

The captain talked until Miss Graveley had all the facts and could see. When he had finished she said: 'You know, Captain, when I ran away I decided not to tell a soul what had happened – it's an undignified thing to happen to a woman of my years –'

'Not at all –' the captain began. Then: 'I mean, you're not at all old. I mean ...' He trailed off, his words miserably inadequate for expressing what he did mean. Then he lit his pipe and sat there saying nothing.

'I was saying,' said Miss Graveley, 'when I ran away I decided not to tell anyone what had occurred. Then I met you and thought how convenient it was that you should think you had shot him – you must forgive me for thinking that.'

'Only natural,' said the captain.

'And that's why I felt so grateful to you,' she said. 'I felt – I still feel – under an obligation to you.'

'Not at all,' said the captain. 'Let's forget it.'

'No, no!' she exclaimed. 'We mustn't do that. It would hardly be fair to you – I mean for you to go through life knowing you'd buried a man you didn't kill. You would have my crime on your conscience –'

'It's a pleasure, I'm sure,' said the captain.

'But no! Now I realize that man was out of his mind and that my action was justifiable, there's no reason why we should not let the authorities know –'

'The authorities?' The captain looked at his companion in sharp alarm. The thought of digging Harry up again made him perspire.

'Then the whole matter will be disposed of nicely,' said Miss Graveley, 'I'm sure the police won't make a fuss about it when we all explain. Perhaps it needn't get into the papers at all –'

'Don't you believe it, ma'am!' the captain exploded at last. 'They love it, the papers, this kind of thing. Murder and adverts, that's what they live on. You let him be. Just forget it ever happened, same as what me and Sammy and Jennifer is going to do.'

'Ah, but it isn't your body,' said Miss Graveley. 'After all, I killed him, so it's only fair I have the say-so –'

'Yes, but –'

'Don't you agree?'

'Yes –'

'I thought you would! I tell you what, Captain Wiles, we'll go and get a spade now –'

'– but –'

'And afterwards,' said Miss Graveley brightly, 'I'll make you some cocoa.'

# Big Things, Trees

Above the bungalows in a small clearing in the thickest part of the wood stood an old barn with a thatched roof. This barn was seldom seen or visited by anyone for there was no real path leading to it and the wood was overgrown with brambles and thickets. The glade in which it stood was just large enough to allow the sunlight to green the grass and the moonlight to flood it with black shadows.

The barn had two windows, both of them clean and bright and thoroughly out of keeping with the old black timber which formed the walls. From the thatch a bent pipe came out at a silly angle; in the winter this pipe sent smoke up through the trees which crowded closely around. It was an ancient building which had been made fit for human habitation.

To this barn, around ten-thirty that night, came Sam Marlow, Jennifer Rogers and Abie. Sam came first, holding the brambles above Jennifer's head and lifting Abie through the darkest and scratchiest patches. At last they stood before the old building and Jennifer was glad there was insufficient light for the artist to observe her true reactions.

'You can't live here!' she exclaimed. 'I had no idea you were a hermit.'

Sam said nothing at once but strode forward and flung open the door. Then, looking back at her, he thumped the doorpost with his fist. 'If your bungalow were half as good and solid as this,' he said. 'If your bungalow had stood for one tenth as long as this,' he said. 'If your lopsided little shed of a place had so much as a splinter of good English timber in it –'

'Sam!' Jennifer joined him in the doorway and laid a hand on his arm, preventing further damage to his fist. 'I'm sorry. Honestly. I had no idea you were in love with the place.'

Sam said: 'Was I shouting at you?'

'A little,' Jennifer said, 'but I asked for it.'

Sam said: 'No, it's me, Jennifer. I've always found it difficult to be polite or sociable for more than ten minutes at a time. I was sent down for pulling the Dean's nose.'

Jennifer waited to hear him laugh, but he didn't. He maintained a sober expression that forced her into laughter. 'How lovely! What a wonderful thing to do.'

'Do you believe that?' Sam said, looking at her almost eagerly.

'Of course I believe it. There must be thousands of people going through life with a miserable repression just because they didn't have the courage to pull the Dean's nose.'

Abie forced his way between their legs and into the barn. Sam and Jennifer followed him. Sam lit a match and applied it to an oil lamp which stood with its tall glass chimney on a rough table.

The room was so large that the light would not go into the remote corners. On the floor, which was built evenly and scientifically of wooden blocks, was a fine and brilliantly coloured carpet. The rough table on which the lamp stood was the sawn bole of a gigantic tree which seemed to be growing out of the floor. Jennifer looked at the room while Sam looked at Jennifer and Abie went exploring.

'What do you think of it now?' Sam asked.

'It's wonderful – like Aladdin's cave,' she said. She looked at the high, beamed roof, the walls smothered in a haphazard yet tasteful fashion with all kinds of paintings and drawings. There were dozens of carvings, too – ships, dogs, men, and women who stood without arms but quite complete in every other respect. 'Wonderful!' she said again. 'You're really awfully clever, Sam. You should make your fortune.'

Sam shrugged. 'I think I have my fortune,' he said. 'Plenty of freedom; plenty of space and trees. Big things, trees. You can sing at the trees, and shout at them. You don't have to be sociable or polite to them. They just stand there and listen and wait . . .'

Jennifer looked speculative. 'But don't you sometimes feel like eating gingerbread, Sam?'

Her question startled him. 'Who, me?'

'Yes.'

'Yes,' he admitted.

Jennifer laughed shortly and ran her fingers through her small son's hair. 'It's funny, but I feel awfully comfortable with you. It's nice to be forthright with somebody as – as forthright as you.'

'Who, me? Forthright?'

'Yes. Talking to you I feel like a character in a novel – you know how forthright they have to be or they'd never get their story over before the last chapter. In real life people spend fifty per cent of their lives hiding what they want to say behind their vocabulary and the other fifty per cent trying to find out what other people are hiding.'

Sam returned her gaze, seriously. He said : 'I like the way you talk and the things you say.'

'Can I have some gingerbread, Mummy?' Abie said, looking up at them and rubbing his eyes.

Jennifer laughed at Sam over the small boy's head. 'It's well beyond his bedtime. I'd better get him home.'

'I'll come with you,' Sam said.

'There's no need,' Jennifer said. 'It's quite late.'

'I want a piggy-back,' Abie said.

'I'll come with you,' Sam said.

# I'll Get My Spade

After Abie had gone to sleep Jennifer made coffee. They were about to drink it when there came an urgent knocking at the door. It was the new captain and Miss Graveley. They came into the room blinking against the light. The captain was shirt-sleeved and perspiring and in one hand he carried a spade.

'What's happened?' Sam asked.

'I've got something to tell you,' said Captain Wiles.

Miss Graveley gripped his arm. 'No, captain. *I* have something to tell them.'

'Make up your minds,' Sam said.

Miss Graveley struck an impressive pose. 'I killed Harry Worp,' she said, 'with my ice-calf brogue.'

Jennifer yawned. She said: 'Oh, him.'

Sam looked at the captain and said: 'Told you so.'

Miss Graveley looked around at them. 'We're on our way to telephone the police,' she said.

Sam and Jennifer sat up and took a great deal of notice.

The captain made an apologetic face behind Miss Graveley's back. 'I keep telling her there's no need. They've got plenty of bodies without this one.'

'You're right,' said Sam. 'It wouldn't be decent. He's dead and buried.'

'He's not, you know,' said the captain, wiping the perspiration from his forehead with his sleeve.

Sam almost gaped. 'You haven't dug him up *again*?'

Miss Graveley intervened. 'I insisted, Mr Marlow. You have nothing to fear. It is my concern entirely. As soon as I heard the full circumstances of his being here I knew there was nothing for me to hide. Nobody could possibly gossip about a lady and a maniac.'

'You'd be surprised,' Sam said. 'I don't think you realize, Miss Graveley, what murder involves – hours and hours of questioning; photographs; the whole of your private life spread indecently in the newspapers.'

'And what makes you think my private life is indecent?' Miss Graveley inquired acidly.

The captain smiled secretly at the artist's embarrassment.

'I didn't mean that. It's the way they pry that's indecent. They'll worry you to death. Policemen, news-reporters, detectives –'

'I have made up my mind,' Miss Graveley said. 'It was the captain who persuaded me to call and tell Mrs Rogers what I proposed doing. After all, she's most closely connected with the business. What do you think about it, Mrs Rogers?'

Jennifer poured two more cups of coffee. 'I can't think why you're making such a fuss about Harry. If he was buried, then I can't see why you had to dig him up. But since you've dug him up, I don't see why you shouldn't do as you think best.' She added: 'Frankly – have some coffee? – I don't care what you do with Harry as long as you don't bring him back to life.'

Miss Graveley accepted the coffee. 'I have a free hand, then?'

'Quite, so far as I'm concerned –'

'Just a minute,' Sam interrupted. 'I think you've forgotten something, Jennifer. If this comes out, do you realize that all the details of your marriage will be public property? Including the origin of Abie?'

'Oh,' Jennifer said.

Miss Graveley looked concerned. 'I must confess, I hadn't thought of that, either.'

The captain sipped his coffee noisily and with relief.

'Where have you put the body this time?' Sam said.

'Top of the heath – near that clump of silver birch,' the captain said.

'I'll get my spade,' Sam said, in a flat, resigned voice.

Miss Graveley sighed. 'I'm afraid I'm causing you rather a lot of hard work. I'm sorry.'

'Not at all,' Sam said.

Jennifer said: 'Let's all go up there. I've never witnessed an unofficial funeral.'

'This is my third.' The captain got to his feet and glanced ruefully at the clock, which now stood at eleven-thirty. 'All in one night, too.'

Presently the four of them were walking the moonlit paths of Sparrowswick Heath looking for Harry. The body was not as easily located as Captain Wiles had implied, there being many clumps of silver birch at the top of the heath. But at last the captain plunged away from them through the heather and bracken and small fir trees.

'Here he is,' he called. 'Come on, you take his feet, Sammy; I'll have his shoulders.'

Sam and the captain carried the body back towards the grave while the women walked behind like a pair of indifferent mourners.

'How about a little service?' the captain suggested, as they held Harry over the deep hole.

'I can't think of anything to say,' Sam said. 'Besides, my arms ache.'

'Drop him in,' Jennifer urged. 'It's too late to say prayers. Wherever he was going he must be there by now.'

# That's Not a Bugle

When they reached the main path on their way home, the still night was suddenly moved by a bugle blast that seemed to come from down beyond the woods.

They stopped. Miss Graveley said: 'Whatever was that?'

'Sounded like the trumpets welcoming Harry,' Captain Wiles said.

'You didn't know Harry,' said Jennifer, her head bent to one side as she listened.

Sam, watching her, said: 'I'd like to paint you like that, Jennifer – you look wonderful standing there, listening in the moonlight.'

She straightened her head and smiled at him. 'What would you call it, Sam?'

Sam considered. 'Just . . . "The Listener". . . . Yes, "The Listener".'

'That's the name of a magazine,' said the captain. 'Think of something original.'

Before Sam could think of anything more, the sound of the bugle notes came to them again.

'I believe it's someone actually up here on the heath,' Sam said. 'It's wonderful, isn't it?'

'I know what it is,' Miss Graveley said. 'It's the call of the phantom stage coach that used to pass by each night two hundred years ago – the old road was right across the top of the heath, you know.'

'Phantom coach?' said the captain, looking at her with his face wrinkled and wondering.

Sam put his face to the sky and swelled his chest with an exultant breath. 'Oh, to be a highwayman on a night like this!'

'Listen!' Jennifer exclaimed. 'Running feet!'

'Horses?' Miss Graveley whispered.

'If it's a horse it's learned how to shout,' Sam commented.

The voice came plainly to them. A voice as thin as the air, bleating out one phrase. A woman's voice.

'What's she saying?' said the captain.

'You'll know in a minute,' Jennifer said. 'She's coming this way – there goes the bugle again!'

'She's calling my name,' said Sam suddenly. 'It's old Wiggy.'

'What, running?' said the captain.

'I'm sure it's Wiggy,' Sam said, his eyes now fixed on the pathway. 'It *is* Wiggy – look, here she comes.'

A strange figure came trotting along the path in the moonlight. She wore a long nightdress which showed white beneath a dressing-gown, and her hair was flying out behind her.

'Mr Marlow! Mr Marlow! Where are you, Mr Marlow?' she called.

Sam stepped into the middle of the path and held up his hand. 'Wiggy! What on earth do you want? Change for sixpence?'

She stopped and looked at the four of them, too breathless, now she had finished shouting, even to talk. She held Sam's arm and pointed back towards the woods. As she pointed the bugle call came as though at her bidding.

Are you having a nightmare?' Sam asked kindly.

'He's a millionaire!' she gasped at last. 'He wants to buy your pictures, Mr Marlow! All of them and more besides. He says you're a genius, Mr Marlow!'

'This is a queer time to come buying pictures,' Sam grumbled.

He looked at Jennifer and the others. Jennifer shrugged, the captain shook his head and Miss Graveley shivered slightly and said: 'Let's go and have some cocoa.'

They started walking towards the woods. As they walked, Sam said: 'What's he blowing a bugle for?'

'That's not a bugle,' Mrs Wiggs said. 'That's the hooter on his car. A great big Rolls-Royce. He drove me right up the estate as far as he could. We've been to your studio, but we couldn't find you anywhere.'

'We've been digging,' Sam explained, making his spade more comfortable on his shoulder.

'It's very good for you is digging,' said Mrs Wiggs. 'My Henry always swore it was that cured his rheumatics.'

'What does this millionaire want to pay?' Sam asked.

'I asked him twelve and six for that bunch of grapes hanging on the swordfish,' Mrs Wiggs said, 'but he said he couldn't think of it. Said they was priceless.'

'Doesn't sound priceless to me,' Captain Wiles remarked. 'Sounds like a pub sign.'

Sam looked down on the little captain. 'That picture is symbolic of the beginning of the world – you know: "He made the earth and the sea and all that in them is".'

'Oh,' said the captain.

'Priceless,' repeated Mrs Wiggs, tripping on her night-dress and clutching at Sam for support.

'I'll find a price for them,' said Sam.

'Ever so took up with them. He got me out of bed by throwing a stone at my window. At first I was angry because I thought he wanted a lemonade, but he told me he stopped by this afternoon and saw the pictures but couldn't wait –'

At that moment a couple emerged from the bracken, attracted by the shouting and the noise. It was Mark Douglas, the landlord and Mrs D'Arcy, the blonde. They were joined almost immediately by yet another couple, who had been sitting in the bracken only a short distance away. These were

Mr Walter D'Arcy and Mrs Mark Douglas. They stood staring at each other.

'Mark!' exclaimed Mrs Douglas.

'My God! Cassy! And with one of my tenants!'

Walter D'Arcy stepped forward and tapped Mark Douglas on the shoulder. He pointed towards the blonde who was looking at him in mingled amazement and delight.

'And that,' said Mr D'Arcy, 'is my wife.'

'Walter!' cried the blonde, stepping forward and throwing her arms around her husband's neck. 'You've been out with a woman!'

'And about time too,' said Walter, nodding.

'I didn't know you had it in you,' said the blonde happily.

'Cassy!' exclaimed Mark Douglas again, his voice filled with pain. 'That you could do a thing like this to me! Me, your husband!'

Suddenly he burst into tears. Then he fled home, weeping noisily. His wife followed him, an expression of triumph on her face, while the D'Arcys stood with their arms around each other, looking after them. Presently they, too, went walking homeward, holding hands and laughing.

Mrs Wiggs said to Sam, just as though nothing had happened to interrupt her: 'And don't shout at him, will you, Mr Marlow? Be nice to him. Perhaps it's the change of your fortune. Don't forget to tell him about your voice, too.'

'What about my voice?'

'The way it sings,' said Mrs Wiggs.

'Why?' said Sam.

'You never know,' said Mrs Wiggs, 'with millionaires.'

# Comes Love

Sam Marlow and his friends stood in the moonlight by the roadside at the foot of the Sparrowswick Bungalow Estate. They could hear the sound of the Rolls-Royce engine decaying into the distance and occasionally the musical, jubilant blare of the electric hooter. All eyes were fastened on a piece of paper which Sam clutched in his hand. It was a cheque for two hundred pounds.

At last, when the engine noise had gone and the hooter was no longer disturbing the night, Sam said: 'Now. Will someone tell me what just happened?'

Mrs Wiggs looked at him uncertainly. Then she said: 'I'll go in and make you a nice cup of tea.'

Sam patted her shoulder. 'Stay, Wiggy. I want someone to repeat what the gentleman said. I want to know if you all heard what I heard.'

'This is the way I heard it,' said Jennifer soberly. 'He said that you are a genius, Sam Marlow. He said your paintings rate with the finest contemporary art. He said he would personally purchase your entire collection and give a private exhibition in London. He said he would give you two hundred pounds for those with Mrs Wiggs and he would be visiting you next week to see the rest.'

Sam nodded at all this, thoughtfully, for it confirmed what he had heard. 'What did I say to that?' he asked.

Jennifer said: 'You agreed you were a genius and you asked him for something on account.'

Sam flicked the cheque with his finger. 'And I got it.'

'And you got it,' Jennifer agreed happily.

'Nice work, Sammy,' said Captain Wiles. 'Very nice indeed.'

'And what are you going to do with your good fortune?' asked Miss Graveley.

'Share it,' said Sam promptly.

'No, no,' Miss Graveley hastened. 'You mustn't be too generous.'

'That's right, Sammy,' said the new captain. 'Got to think about your old age.'

'That's what I'm thinking about,' Sam said. 'I don't mean share it with everybody. I mean share it with a good woman.'

Miss Graveley beamed benevolently. 'How lovely! You're going to marry?'

Jennifer stared at Sam. 'You secretive old thing, Sam. You never told me you had a romance in view.'

Sam shrugged. 'I thought it would be forward of me. After all, I only really met you today.'

'Maybe so,' Jennifer said. 'But the first thing you told me was that I was the most wonderful, beautiful thing you'd ever seen. You might easily have turned my head – or, worse still, made me fall in love with you.'

'Well, why shouldn't you fall in love with me?' said Sam. 'I'm in love with you.'

'Hold hard, Sammy boy,' said the captain. 'Don't let a little dough shatter your sense of responsibility. Here you are talking about marrying somebody and in the next breath you say you're in love with Jennifer.'

'Well,' said Sam, looking half puzzled and half truculent at his companions, 'isn't that the right thing to do? Isn't that the right sequence? First I say I want to get married, then I say I love her –'

'But Mr Marlow –' Miss Graveley began.

'I don't comprehend,' the captain admitted frankly.

Sam turned to Jennifer. 'Do you, Jennifer?' he asked in one of his softer tones.

Jennifer laughed a little nervously, then stopped and gulped. 'You mean – you want to marry *me*?'

Sam tapped the cheque on his hand. 'Why not?'

'But . . .' Jennifer searched her mind for some objection. 'I've only just got my freedom,' she said at last. 'Just to-day.'

Sam shrugged. 'Easy come, easy go,' he said. 'Besides, if you married me you would keep your freedom.'

Jennifer found a smile. 'You must be practically unique then!'

'I respect freedom,' said Sam. 'More: I love freedom. We would probably be the only free married couple in the world.'

Jennifer stared at the moon as though for guidance. Then she said:

'This is very sudden. You'll have to give me a little time, Sam.'

'Only fair,' said Sam reasonably. 'I'll give you till we get back to your bungalow.'

Mrs Wiggs gave up. 'I think I'll go back to bed,' she said levelly, in a tone which implied that bed at least was something she could understand and appreciate.

'You do that, Wiggy,' said Sam, 'and tomorrow I'll give you your ten per cent.'

'Good night, Mr Marlow,' said Mrs Wiggs, fading into the shadows of the ivy on the Emporium wall so effectively that none of them was sure she had ever been there.

When they arrived back at Jennifer's bungalow for supper Jennifer laid her hand on Sam's arm.

'I've decided, Sam,' she said.

Sam looked at her expectantly. The new captain and Miss Graveley stopped at the gate behind them, waiting to hear Jennifer's decision.

Jennifer said: 'I think I will marry you, Sam, if you don't mind. I'm fond of you; we have a great deal in common, and Abie needs a father.'

Sam put his arms around her with an air of enjoyment.

'Then I can kiss you?'

'Yes, please,' Jennifer said, closing her eyes.

'What a pretty sight!' said Miss Graveley.

The captain ran his tongue around his teeth in a speculative manner as he watched the young couple embracing. He was remembering the bells he had heard that afternoon, and wondering if they had been in his head or in Sam's.

Sam and Jennifer stood apart feeling pleased and satisfied and looking at each other as though viewing a new and delightful acquisition. Miss Graveley and the captain thrust themselves forward.

'Congratulations, my dear,' said Miss Graveley, kissing Jennifer lightly on the cheek. 'What a neat arrangement!'

'You're a lucky man, Sammy,' said the captain, wringing the artist's hand. 'I think you'll be very happy together, up here in the woods like two love birds. And if I grumbled at all at my share of the work in burying Harry, then I'm sorry, for now I can see it was well worth it. If there's anything else I can do for you two, I'm more than willing to lend a hand –'

'Hold it!' said Sam, withdrawing his hand and putting on a thoughtful expression.

'What's up, Sam?' Jennifer said.

'Harry,' said Sam. 'I'm afraid we haven't finished with him yet, sweetheart.'

'I don't understand,' Jennifer said. 'If anybody's finished Harry is – he's been buried three times.'

'Before we can marry,' Sam said gently, 'you'll have to prove that you're free; to prove you're free you'll have to prove that Harry –'

'– is dead,' Jennifer finished. 'What a horrid complication!'

'Oh, I don't know that it is,' Miss Graveley said, looking at Captain Wiles expectantly.

'What are you looking at me for?' said the captain with

alarm. 'I'll do anything to help you, Sammy, but please, please don't ask me to dig up Harry again!'

'Come, come now,' Miss Graveley said reproachfully.

'No,' Jennifer said, grasping Sam's arm. 'We can't do that.'

'If you're thinking of the publicity on your first unfortunate love affair –' began Miss Graveley.

'I'm not,' said Jennifer. 'I think Sam would be worth anything. I'm thinking of you, Miss Graveley. Murder is murder no matter how exonerating the circumstances, and it wouldn't be at all nice for you.'

'That's right,' said the captain. 'Better let him stay where he is. You only have to wait seven years to presume death, anyway –'

'Seven years!' groaned Sam. 'I'll be an old man!'

'Don't be silly, Sam,' Jennifer told him. 'You've waited far longer than seven years already.'

Sam looked at her appraisingly. 'Yes, but now I know what I'm waiting for,' he said.

'I insist you dig the wretched man up,' said Miss Graveley. 'I don't care a jot what they say to me. They'll only have to look at me to know the man must have been mad.'

'I disagree!' said the captain emphatically.

They looked at him. The captain looked at his feet and shuffled.

'Really, Captain Wiles?' Miss Graveley said, pleasantly.

The captain squared his shoulders. His heart was racing at an unusual speed for there had been something almost encouraging in Miss Graveley's face and voice at that moment. 'I'll dig him up,' he said.

# This Is Ridiculous

At one a.m. the four people and the two spades made their way once more to the grave in the bracken. The heath at this hour was completely out of the world. The moon had crimsoned and swollen and was falling after the sun; between the trees and over the bracken and the shrubbery there lay the faint suspicion of a mist. It brought a thin chill to the air and lent an aspect of fairies and goblins and film sets.

Now Miss Graveley and Jennifer, wearing their coats across their shoulders like cloaks, stood in the darkness watching the captain and Sam disinter Harry for the third time.

Jennifer said suddenly: 'I've been thinking.'

The men went on digging and Miss Graveley went on watching.

'I've been thinking,' Jennifer said, 'that maybe we could forget the way it really happened.'

Sam stopped digging and looked across at her. Miss Graveley looked at her. The captain went on digging.

'I could tell how he visited me today and then went off in a temper. That's all we need know of him being here,' Jennifer said.

Miss Graveley had been considering all the possibilities and now she shook her head. 'No. Somebody else might get the blame. And somebody else might not have such a good motive as I did. After all, you are allowed to kill in self-defence, aren't you?'

Sam began pushing his spade into the ground again. 'I wouldn't worry about somebody else getting the blame,' he said. 'It could only be attributed to some person or persons unknown, the way it often happens.'

'How do you know that?' Miss Graveley asked. 'I can think of at least two people on this heath with a good motive for having killed Harry.'

Sam stopped digging and this time so did the captain.

'Go on,' said Jennifer.

Miss Graveley smiled apologetically. 'I'm only thinking of what the police would call a motive – first you, Jennifer, because you were married to him.'

'That's certainly a good motive,' Jennifer agreed.

'And so is Sam's,' Miss Graveley said. 'Now.'

'Mine?' said Sam. 'Why would I want to kill him? I never met him.'

'You didn't have to meet him to have a motive for killing him,' Miss Graveley said gently.

'She means me,' Jennifer said. 'Don't you, Miss Graveley?'

Miss Graveley bowed her head slightly. 'Of course.'

Sam gave a short, unconvincing laugh. 'But I didn't fall in love with Jennifer till after Harry was dead.'

'Try telling that to the police,' said Miss Graveley.

'She's right, Sammy boy,' the captain contributed. 'You've both been living up here in the woods a long time . . .'

Jennifer said: 'On second thoughts we'd better stick to the truth.'

The men went on digging and a reflective silence fell upon the group. Soon they were scraping the last of the earth away from Harry with their hands. They dragged him out of the hole and laid him alongside.

Harry's face was fixed coldly on the cold sky, and mingled with the tang of the earth they could detect the scent of his hair oil.

'Ugh!' said Jennifer.

Sam put his arm around her, then he said: 'We'll have

to get the story right. Times and so forth. If it happened early afternoon we'll have to think of some reason why the police weren't informed before now. Then there's the mess he's in – that'll take some explaining.'

'We'll have to clean him up,' Jennifer said. 'It's horrible, but there's nothing else for it. We can't risk complicating Miss Graveley's confession.'

'And as for the delay,' Miss Graveley said, 'I can explain that I was so upset by the occurrence that I went straight home and rested.'

'Only natural,' said the captain.

'They'll think you rested a long time,' Sam commented doubtfully.

'That's all right,' Jennifer said. 'Miss Graveley can tell them that she was too frightened to say anything about it, but when she got to bed she found it was preying on her mind so she got up, dressed, and came down to ask my advice –'

'They'll think it a bit of a coincidence, won't they? – I mean, since he was your husband?' Sam asked.

Jennifer bit her lip, thinking. The new captain grabbed Harry's feet suddenly and said: 'Well, come on, we'd best get him down to the bungalows if we're going to clean him up. P'raps we'll think of a good story on the way down.'

Sam took Harry by the shoulders and the little procession got under way. They walked slowly and tiredly along the heath path and the mist swirled around them. Under the big oak tree near the top of the bungalow path they put their burden down on the dewy grass and squatted for a rest.

'He seems to get heavier all the time,' Sam complained, taking out a half of a cigarette while the captain thumbed his pipe bowl.

'Listen!' Miss Graveley exclaimed. 'Somebody's coming!'

103

'Hide the body!' Sam exclaimed. 'Quickly!'

'Too late,' said the captain. 'Put your cigarette in his mouth, Sammy – go on!'

Sam hesitated only for a moment, then he stooped and thrust the glowing cigarette between the cold, stiff lips. All four of them ducked into the bracken.

A man came along the path. He came slowly, as though he were out for a leisurely constitutional. When he got close, the captain recognized the tramp who had spat in Harry's eye and stolen his socks and shoes earlier in the day. This tramp was holding a conversation with himself, and it seemed to the watchers that he might not notice Harry at all. But Harry's bare feet were spread across the path and the tramp kicked them. He swore, stooped, and looked down into Harry's face. He kicked Harry again, then, satisfied, he reached out his hand and plucked the smouldering cigarette stub from Harry's mouth and put it into his own.

Sam, watching from the bracken, quivered, and it was only Jennifer's restraining hand that kept him from leaping out to object to this acquisition of his property.

When the tramp had moved on, mumbling something from Virgil, Sam and the others came out and watched him out of sight.

'People like that,' said Miss Graveley, 'have no sense of decency.'

'Take Harry's feet,' Sam said to the captain.

The captain went to obey but immediately there came the sound of more footsteps, this time hurrying.

'This is ridiculous!' said Jennifer crossly. 'No respectable people walk abroad at one o'clock in the morning.'

They had no time to plan anything before the newcomer was upon them. He was a tall, thin man, carrying a canvas bag under his arm and a butterfly net over his shoulder. He was walking quickly with his head down.

'Dr Greenbow!' said Jennifer.

'Crikey!' said the captain. 'That butterfly must have

given him a chase. I last saw him about eight hours ago, disappearing in a nor'-nor'-east direction.'

'Good evening,' said Sam politely when the doctor reached them.

But the doctor did not reply for he was fast asleep. Before they could do anything he had tripped over the body of Harry and fallen flat, his net prodding the captain in the stomach and his bag tumbling open on the ground. He sat up immediately, as one well used to being aroused from deep sleep into skilled alertness.

'Hello!' he said, his eyes wide open.

Sam stepped forward and helped the doctor to his feet. The doctor looked at Harry and said: 'I beg your pardon; most careless of me –' He broke off and looked around him, sudden panic showing in his eyes. 'My Painted Lady! Where is she? What happened to my Painted Lady?'

'You tell us,' the captain suggested.

'She's escaping!' The doctor leaped up suddenly and made a dive for his bag. He was just too late. A large and beautiful butterfly, smothered in gay colours, emerged shyly from the bag and took flight; it flew tentatively, experimentally, as though unused to late hours. It fluttered drunkenly away across the bracken and by a trick of moonlight and mist it was suddenly gone.

With a heartbroken cry the doctor began to follow, then he stood still, uncertain, straining his eyes in several directions, his thin head bobbing like a turkey searching for worms.

'What happened to her?' he asked miserably, turning back to the others.

'Somebody switched her off,' said the captain.

The doctor groaned and came back to the path, collecting his bag and net. 'All day,' he crooned. 'All day I've been chasing her.'

'You haven't been chasing her all night as well, have you?' asked the captain.

'Practically. I caught her just ten minutes and fifteen seconds past nine o'clock,' said the doctor, climbing sorrowfully to his feet. 'And I was so tired I went to sleep. I was miles from home. Then I woke up and found it was late and began to walk. I must have gone to sleep while I was walking. I don't remember getting this far. I'm really very tired. Extremely tired.'

'How very unfortunate,' Miss Graveley commiserated. 'Perhaps you will find her again tomorrow.'

'If I do it will finish me,' the doctor said. 'I'm quite exhausted.' He glanced down at Harry. 'So is your friend apparently.'

Sam and the captain exchanged a glance; Sam nodded. The captain said:

'Would you mind looking at him, doctor? We think he's met with a bit of an accident.'

The doctor stooped and felt Harry's pulse, absently. His gaze wandered tiredly across the bracken, still in search of the Painted Lady. He was silent for so long they thought he had fallen asleep again. Presently Sam nudged him in the back.

'How about Harry?' he asked.

'He's dead,' said the doctor impersonally. 'Been dead a long time.'

'Do you think it was accidental?' Sam asked.

The doctor raised a thin finger. 'How can I tell? Death is so often an accident.'

'But can't you tell us just how he died?' Sam persisted.

The doctor yawned and tapped his hand on his mouth politely.

'Suppose we take him to where there's more light,' he suggested.

'Good idea,' Sam said. 'Come, Captain, take his feet.'

# As Good As New

Just after one a.m. they filed into 'Chaos'. And sitting in an armchair was Abie, a pistol in his hand and a brave, defensive glitter in his eyes. As Sam entered the room Abie squirted him with a jet of milk from the gun.

'Abie!' Jennifer said, going quickly across to him. 'Whatever are you doing?'

'I woke up,' Abie said. 'I heard someone crying and I woke up.'

Jennifer looked at Sam. 'That must have been Mr Douglas.'

'Then I heard someone laughing and I woke up again,' said Abie.

'Mr and Mrs D'Arcy,' said Sam.

Abie looked with faint curiosity at the body of Harry as they placed him on the sofa. His young memory stirred at the sight of the dead, familiar face. 'Get up, you brute,' he said. He redirected the pistol and a jet of milk went on to Harry's face.

'Abie!' said Jennifer, catching the look of mild surprise on the doctor's face. 'You mustn't do that. The gentleman's dead.'

'He's a brute,' Abie said sullenly, reaching across to replenish his pistol from the milk jug on the table.

The doctor knelt down by the body and the others gathered around.

'H'm,' said Doctor Greenbow, wiping some black soil from Harry's face.

'What's the verdict?' the captain asked.

Miss Graveley shivered delicately. 'Don't use those words, please, Captain Wiles,' she said.

'He's dead,' said the doctor. 'Been dead some time.'

'We know that,' Jennifer said. 'Can't you tell us how he died?'

Sam, Jennifer, Captain Wiles and Miss Graveley exchanged anxious glances. Although they had decided to make a full confession, they were not eager to begin. Besides, this encounter with the doctor had complicated matters. They would now have to fashion their story to explain the midnight frolic with the dead man.

'It was his heart,' said the doctor. 'He had a seizure. This hot weather –'

Sam's mouth opened and nothing came out.

'His heart?' said Jennifer.

'A seizure?' said Miss Graveley with immense relief.

'Well, I'll go to sea!' said the new captain. 'Death from natural causes!' He sank into a chair and sagged back.

Jennifer was looking at the corpse in disbelief. 'But he always boasted he never saw a doctor in his life!'

'More's the pity, my dear,' said the doctor, getting to his feet. 'If he had he might have been alive now.'

'What an awful thought!' Jennifer exclaimed.

The doctor misunderstood her. He got to his feet and held her arm in a professionally sympathetic manner. 'Did you know him?'

Jennifer nodded. 'I was his wife,' she admitted.

The doctor looked at Abie and his face lengthened several inches. 'I'm really deeply sorry,' he intoned, 'for you and the little man.'

Abie squinted his eye along the barrel of his gun and took careful aim. As the jet of milk went into Harry's face again he said: 'Get up, you brute.'

The doctor looked hard at Abie, then rubbed his eyes. Suddenly he looked around at the others and his face was broken by a cavernous grin. He said, with sudden understanding: 'Do you know, this is the first nightmare I've had in years.'

Sam popped his fingers to his ears and waggled them at the doctor while the others regarded him disconcertedly. He extended his hand to the staring medico. 'Come, let's go find the Painted Lady,' he suggested.

The doctor grabbed his net and his bag and joined Sam at the door. 'The Painted Lady,' he said eagerly. 'The Painted Lady!'

Sam led him out of the bungalow and up the woodland path, leaving the others staring after them. 'The bit you'll enjoy most when you wake up,' he said, as they walked, 'is where the little boy squirted milk at the corpse.'

'Yes,' said the doctor, giggling happily. 'Yes, yes, yes . . .'

By the time Sam returned, 'Chaos' had the appearance of a steam laundry. Harry was stretched out on the table, his trousers were in the kitchen being sponged by Miss Graveley, his coat was being pressed by Jennifer, and the captain was fitting on him a pair of his own shoes.

Sam stood inside the door and looked approvingly at all this industry. 'I see you got my point,' he said.

Jennifer took his arm. 'I think I've got an awfully clever fiancé,' she claimed. 'I was beginning to puzzle how we could explain things to the doctor. I wonder how he could tell it was Harry's heart.'

'Look at his face now I've washed it,' Miss Graveley said. 'It's blue!'

'He *must* have got excited,' Sam commented.

Jennifer said: 'He was too late. He should have got excited years ago.'

Miss Graveley bustled out of the room again, saying: 'Well, come along. Let's finish him off.'

'What are you going to do?' Sam asked.

'Put him back where we found him,' Jennifer said, 'and let Abie find him again tomorrow.'

'Then what?' Sam asked.

'Abie will come down here and tell me; I'll phone the police, and everyone will be happy.'

'What about the cut on his head?' Sam said, viewing the body critically.

'I've thought of that,' said Miss Graveley, coming into the room with Harry's trousers. 'I'm going to put some plaster on it, then they'll think it was done before he died.'

Sam nodded approvingly. 'I think that covers everything,' he said.

'Then let's cover Harry,' suggested the captain. He took the trousers from Miss Graveley and she went quickly into the kitchen again in search of sticking-plaster.

Soon they sat eating supper while Abie lay gently snoring in the next room and Harry lay clean, polished, brushed and dead on the sofa.

# Another Day

The small boy named Abie climbed the woodland path that led to Sparrowswick Heath. His body lay at an acute angle with the steep and stony way, a toy gun was clutched firmly beneath his left arm.

He left the dark tunnel of the woodland path for the broad paths of the heath. Splendid paths bordered by a tangle of blue heather and wild snapdragons; paths where rabbits could hop when the sun went out and where hares could race recklessly yet safely on bright mornings. Also a million little paths that darted and flitted and curled and twisted and climbed and tumbled about all over the place without any definite plan or notion. Paths to lead the unwary into an entanglement of brambles, or sweethearts into quiet places. They led Abie to Harry.

When he saw the corpse lying there he was surprised and annoyed because he clearly remembered coming across it before; was it tomorrow, or just now? He didn't know. The man was sprawled on his back and Abie nearly stepped on him. A big man with a moustache and wavy hair. On his forehead there was a neatly-cut piece of sticking-plaster and in his breast-pocket was a newly-ironed white handkerchief. He was a most immaculate corpse.

Abie hesitated before turning back. He stooped and tried to lift the body by the shoulders, but found it impossible. He stood there, undecided.

On the opposite side of the path, hidden by the bracken and shrubbery, three people were staring anxiously at the small boy, trying to will him to run home and tell his mother. These three were Captain Albert Wiles, Miss Graveley and Sam Marlow. Eventually Abie did reluctantly turn and plod towards home, his gun at the trail.

When he had gone the new captain turned to his companions and winked, putting his thumbs up expressively. Sam smiled and beckoned them out on to the path.

They stood for a moment in silent farewell of the body.

Miss Graveley turned to the new captain and there was a happy light in her eyes. 'What is your first name, Captain Wiles?' she asked.

'Albert,' said Captain Wiles.

'Albert,' said Miss Graveley, 'take my arm.'

Captain Wiles took her arm and cocked his head to one side. 'Can you hear them bells?' he asked joyfully.

'They're not bells,' Sam said, leading the way into the woods. 'I have an orchestra in my head – listen!'

He sang: '*I want to carve your name on every tree . . .*'

Soon they were gone, but the song remained on the heath. It dwelt in the bracken and the grassy glades; it soared through the highest branches of the trees and it whispered amongst the blue heather, gladdening the hearts of all the little creatures.